F250

P9-CLR-630

An unwelcome guest . . .

Rebecca pulled a small suitcase from the back seat, then followed me inside.

"Wow!" she said, looking around the living room. "This is like a mansion or something." I must have frowned a little. "You people are rich. I didn't know rich black people existed except on the Cosbys. But that's television." She put her bag down and walked over to the fish tank. She was a little clumsy because she leaned forward slightly to hide her stomach. "Look at this!" she said. "Look at all those fishes."

"Fish."

She straightened up and turned to me, her eyebrows meeting at the center of her forehead. "Look! Just 'cause I'm in your ritzy little house," she hissed, "doesn't mean you gonna teach me how to talk and tell me what to do. I don't want to be in this mansion in the boring country nohow! You think you special or something, but I know all about you, Feni Harris. Your mama says you don't talk to nobody and you don't have any friends. So you better consider yourself lucky that I'm here, whether I'm here saying 'fishes,' 'fish,' or 'fried fish'!" She put her hands on her hips and stared at me.

"The word is still *fish*," I said, taking the groceries into the kitchen.

❧

"The book rises above the limits of a problem novel by offering portraits of richly developed characters and a satisfying emotional conclusion."   —*The Horn Book*

"Woodson's deep understanding of and concern for the role of black women in society is evident . . . in her moving, powerful story."   —*Publishers Weekly*

JACQUELINE WOODSON

the dear one

PUFFIN BOOKS
An Imprint of Penguin Group (USA) Inc.

PUFFIN BOOKS
Published by the Penguin Group
Penguin Young Readers Group, 345 Hudson Street, New York, New York 10014, U.S.A.
Penguin Group (Canada), 90 Eglinton Avenue East, Suite 700, Toronto, Ontario, Canada M4P 2Y3
(a division of Pearson Penguin Canada Inc.)
Penguin Books Ltd, 80 Strand, London WC2R 0RL, England
Penguin Ireland, 25 St Stephen's Green, Dublin 2, Ireland (a division of Penguin Books Ltd)
Penguin Group (Australia), 250 Camberwell Road, Camberwell, Victoria 3124, Australia
(a division of Pearson Australia Group Pty Ltd)
Penguin Books India Pvt Ltd, 11 Community Centre,
Panchsheel Park, New Delhi - 110 017, India
Penguin Group (NZ), 67 Apollo Drive, Rosedale, North Shore 0632, New Zealand
(a division of Pearson New Zealand Ltd)
Penguin Books (South Africa) (Pty) Ltd, 24 Sturdee Avenue,
Rosebank, Johannesburg 2196, South Africa

Registered Offices: Penguin Books Ltd, 80 Strand, London WC2R 0RL, England

First published in the United States of America by Delacorte Press, 1991
Published by G. P. Putnam's Sons, a division of Penguin Putnam Books for Young Readers, 2003
Published by Speak, an imprint of Penguin Group (USA) Inc., 2004
This edition published by Puffin Books, a division of Penguin Young Readers Group, 2010

CIP DATA IS AVAILABLE

Puffin Books ISBN: 978-0-14-241705-8

1 3 5 7 9 10 8 6 4 2

Copyright © Jacqueline Woodson, 1991
All rights reserved

Printed in the United States of America

Except in the United States of America, this book is sold subject to the condition
that it shall not, by way of trade or otherwise, be lent, re-sold, hired out, or otherwise
circulated without the publisher's prior consent in any form of binding or cover
other than that in which it is published and without a similar condition
including this condition being imposed on the subsequent purchaser.

The publisher does not have any control over and does not assume
any responsibility for author or third-party Web sites or their content.

*For my readers at MS 51 and
New Voices Middle School*

ONE THING I LEARNED FROM REBECCA IS THAT WHEN people talk about fifteen-year-olds who are pregnant, they never mention anything about the lost look in the girls' eyes. Rebecca said those people talking and writing books and articles don't know what's really going on. They don't know that a lot of times, the girls don't even take all their clothes off. They don't know that romance is out the window like time flying, and sometimes the kids are so into listening out, making sure nobody's coming up the stairs, that they miss all the action right there in the bedroom or the corner of the kitchen, or the closet—wherever they are. Rebecca told me that. In the same breath she explained how she couldn't wait to get with Danny, how she loved the closeness, loved being loved by him. She said there's something you can't explain about that feeling, least to a twelve-year-old. How could anyone who's never met Rebecca know anything about what it's like to be fifteen with your back pressed against a cold wall, listening . . . listening, hoping nobody catches you in such an embarrassing position? Rebecca said sometimes you're so scared. But she could never come up with a word to describe just how scary it is.

My grandmother once told me that all it takes is for one tiny thing to happen and then, Boom! your life is changed forever. That's what I'm trying to remember now—the one tiny thing. The thing that might have happened to Rebecca before she came, the thing that happened to me after she was here. Because by the time she left, we were different people, all of us—her, me, Ma—even Marion.

Grandma said if I ever want to remember stuff about anything in the past, then I have to go back as far as I can, reach down as deep as I can, even if all that reaching and remembering hurts sometimes. She said only after I've gathered it all up can I make sense out of it. Grandma told me that if I hold on to stuff, I can tell it to my children and they can grow up stronger.

One

THE SKY WAS THE PALEST PINK THE DAY I TURNED twelve. Sitting on the ledge of my window, I watched blue jays and cardinals flutter by, their wings black against the little bit of light in the sky, black against the bare trees forming skeletons up and down the block, black against the pale patches of February snow.

"Why'd you have to be born in the winter?" my friend Caesar had asked me at lunch the previous week. "Winters are too cold, too still, for anybody to be born in."

I had looked at Caesar for a long time and thought of the word we had learned in English class just the day before. *Profound.*

"That's a profound question, Caesar," I'd said, liking the way the sentence rolled off my tongue. Feeling proud and profound. Caesar had giggled. Giggles come easily to her. "You're right, though," I'd said. "Winter's such a dead season."

And sitting on the windowsill, I thought of the question and counted back. If I was a February baby, then Ma and Dad would have had to have done it in April or May.

3

Maybe Ma found out that she was pregnant in one of those months. Maybe she and Dad hadn't started fighting a whole lot yet. If it was a weekend when the doctor gave her the news, maybe she set out the good silverware and china, lit two candles on the dining-room table, and made Dad fettuccine with broccoli in a red sauce. Maybe the two of them held hands across the table when she told him, and maybe he came around to her side of the table and hugged her long and hard when he realized he was going to be a daddy. Maybe he laughed so hard, tears came into his eyes.

Clair phoned at six in the morning. At first I thought it was Caesar calling to tell me she wouldn't be at school because of the snow. But then I heard Ma say softly, out of breath, "Oh, Clair, it's you. It's been so long." After a pause she added, "Too long."

Outside, the snow had left a thin white sheet over the trees, and I knew the day would be cold and bright. I tiptoed to the top of the stairs, hid behind the banister, and listened.

"But what about the father?" I heard Ma say. There was silence. "Well," Ma said after a long time, "I really want to do this. It would be wonderful having Rebecca here. But what about Feni?"

"What *about* me?" I wanted to scream.

"We'll have to see how it works out," Ma said. "When is she due?"

More silence. I was crouched low in the darkness and the backs of my knees were beginning to hurt.

"Well, I'm touched that you're asking me to do this. And you're right, I think it would be good for Feni. Look, I should be home around five. I'll talk to her then," Ma said. She sounded tired. "Right now, I have to make a meeting before work." Ma laughed nervously. "I've stopped drinking, you know. Yes, it *is* hard but I'm doing it. One day at a time," she said. "It's so good to hear your voice too. . . ."

Ma and Clair talked for a few more minutes. When she hung up, I leaned back against the wall and pulled my knees to my chin. Somebody was coming to stay with us. Sitting against the wall, I wondered who that somebody was.

I heard Ma dialing and leaned against the banister again.

"Marion," she said, "I guess Clair's called you too." She sighed. "Well, I'm going to talk to her about it tonight. Are you coming for dinner? . . . Good! We can all talk. Eight o'clock is fine. See you then."

When I heard Ma heading toward the kitchen, I tip-toed back to my room and climbed underneath the com-forter. It is blue with pink roses. My father had it sent to me from Colorado, where he lives now with his new wife and baby daughter. He left three years ago when I was nine. I used to think about him every day. Sometimes I would come home thinking he'd be sitting in his favorite chair, the brown leather one in the living room next to the fireplace. I'd see him there reading the newspaper and smoking a pipe. I'd think that as soon as I opened the door, the cherry-sweet smell of his tobacco would fill up my nose and mouth and Dad would say, "Let me take a look at what schoolwork Roper Academy is sending home these days." I'd see myself coming over to him with my coat still on, handing him last night's homework or that day's test, and he'd pat me on the arm or hug me real quick and say, "Smartest girl in the school, aren't you? That must come from *my* side of the family." Then maybe he'd laugh, scratch a five-o'clock-shadow kiss against my cheek, set up the chessboard, and show me how to play a fool's game, capturing my opponent's king in six moves or less.

But now when I come home at the end of the day, the house doesn't smell like anything but maybe a little bit of something we had for dinner last night or one of Marion's cigarettes.

Last August I went to visit him and his new wife, Joanne. Joanne is about a foot shorter than my dad and as round as a Thanksgiving turkey. She was constantly nibbling on something or sitting down to a three-course meal, claiming the baby she was three months pregnant with kept her eating. She had stopped working after she married Dad.

"I always wanted to be barefoot and pregnant." She would laugh, winking at me like we were in on some secret together.

Dad rushed around helping her from one chair to another, from the bedroom to the bathroom, as though she were an invalid. They walked the streets holding hands.

I stayed two weeks. And although Dad and I played chess, took walks full of long silences through Denver, and kissed each other hello and good-bye, the smell of his pipe was all that was familiar about him now. We talked around things the way strangers did.

When Ma woke me up again later, I had nearly forgotten about the call.

"Happy birthday, baby."

Ma was sitting at the foot of my bed. On her lap was a box wrapped with a yellow bow. On top of that sat a smaller box wrapped with a green one. Ma smiled. Sun streamed through a slit in the curtain and settled on her face. Her skin is dark brown and smooth everywhere but on her forehead, where wrinkles creep across. Her eyes are so dark, they look black beneath her lashes. There is a small pink spot at the center of her bottom lip. She says the spot was left by vodka. Every time she sees it, she tells herself, *I don't need a drink today.* Ma stopped drinking right after Dad left and says the spot will keep her from ever drinking again. A beauty mark on her right cheek becomes the head of an arrow when she smiles.

"Happy birthday," she said again, and reached to give me a hug. She smelled like sandalwood soap.

I opened the small box first and found a square of silver. Pressing my nails into the small split on the side, I opened it and it became a framed picture of Grandma. In the picture she was about my age. Her eyes looked right at me and smiled. I swallowed. She was holding a small dog. The dog was looking at Grandma. I held the picture close to me. "Where did you get it?"

"It was with a lot of pictures in the attic. I found it a while back and knew it would be perfect. Do you like it?"

I nodded and looked at the picture again. Grandma was still looking at me.

"Open this one," Ma said. "Happy birthday to you . . . ," she sang, her voice soft and clear. "Happy birthday to you. Happy birthday, dear Afeni . . ."

There must have been a hundred sheets of tissue paper in the second box. At the bottom was a smaller box the color of cement. I opened it slowly. Inside was a pewter mountain with an amethyst moon sitting on top. I touched the stone. It was dark purple in some places, nearly transparent in others. "It's beautiful, Ma . . . ," I said, holding the stone up toward the window. Purple rays shot through it onto my hand. "Beautiful."

Ma gave me another hug before she rose. We looked at each other for a moment. Her eyes were proud. "Get up now, birthday girl. I'm going to have to drive you to school before I go to work."

When I got out of the shower, the phone was ringing again. This time I knew who it was.

"Happy birthday to you," Dad sang through the distance, static muffling the words.

"Hi," I said.

"Did you get my present?"

"The mailman hasn't passed."

"I miss you, Feni. When are you coming out to Colorado again?"

"I don't know. Sometime . . . I guess."

"Are you having a good birthday?"

"Yes, thank you."

"I can't believe you're thirteen today."

"I'm not. I'm twelve."

He laughed nervously. "Of course you're twelve. What else would you be? How's your mama?"

"Fine. How's your Joanne?"

"She's fine. Your mama tell you you have a new little sister? Her name's Charisse."

"Yes."

"She'll be a month on the eighteenth. She's something else!"

"That's nice."

"Well, I guess I'll let you go enjoy your birthday. Eat some cake for me, sweetheart. I miss you."

"Bye, Dad." I held on to the phone after we'd said good-bye.

"Feni!" Ma yelled from the kitchen. I jumped. "Is that Bernard on the phone?"

"It was."

"Did he hang up already?"

"Yes."

"My goodness, that was quick. Well . . . come on downstairs so I can fix you up a little before we leave."

The soft click-clack of her heels faded as she passed through the kitchen into the den.

In the kitchen I poured Cheerios into a yellow bowl with blue flowers dancing around it and carried it into the den.

Ma was sitting at her desk, wearing a dark blue suit and

glasses. The glasses were stylish, but thick. Sometimes she wore contact lenses, but most of the time she didn't want to deal with them. Her briefcase was spilled out over everything.

"Hey, honey," she said, not looking up from a page of figures.

I sat on the edge of the leather chair she'd bought for herself on her thirty-fifth birthday, careful not to spill my breakfast. Ma and her best friend, Marion, had the exact same birthday—August 11, 1960. It was fun celebrating two birthdays at one time, but it left me pretty broke. Marion's girlfriend, Bernadette, had the same complaint.

"Why'd someone call so early?" I asked, shoveling a spoonful of cereal into my mouth.

"That was Clair. You remember her, don't you? Me and Marion's friend from college?"

"Yeah, I remember her. But why'd she call?"

Ma scribbled some figures onto her pad, checked them on a calculator, and scribbled something else. She frowned, lifted her glasses to rub her eyes. For the past six years she has been the vice president of a public-relations firm— working sixty to seventy hours a week.

"I'll tell you about it on the way to school," Ma said, looking up. "Don't you want to iron that shirt, Feni? After all, it is your birthday."

The wrinkled shirt I was wearing had a button missing at the bottom. The head of the alligator emblem on the chest pocket was half gone.

"No."

10

"What about that nice skirt I bought you, the long one with the stripes?"

"I don't want to wear a skirt today."

Ma frowned, and the wrinkles buckling across her forehead made her look old. "You have to start caring a little more about the way you look," she said. "You're getting too old to dress like that."

I bent down to tie my worn hiking boots. "I'm ready," I said quickly, holding the brush out to her. She closed her briefcase and I sat on the floor with my head leaning against her leg. She pulled the brush through my hair a few times before wrapping it into a tight French braid down the back of my head. But when I looked into the mirror, my hair was already starting to frizz out around my forehead.

"Are you coming straight home?" Ma asked, following me into the hall and pulling on her coat.

"Yeah. You said I didn't have to go to Jack and Jill, since it's my birthday." I zipped up my ski jacket and wrapped a scarf around my head.

"I know, I know."

"That club's such a pain, Ma. The only cool person in it is Caesar."

"What's wrong with the rest of the kids?"

"All the girls want to do is talk about boys, and all the boys want to do is bother the girls. Everybody thinks they're so special because their parents have good jobs."

"Black professionals are special, Feni. The kids should be proud of who they are."

"Yeah, being proud is one thing, but being out-and-out

11

snobs is a pain. They sit around and talk about how they're going to run the world. I don't have any interest in running anybody's world. I don't care about what shades of makeup go with my skin or what sorority I'm pledging when I get to college. I'm not even in high school!"

"But black kids need a place to meet other black kids. And Jack and Jill was founded to do just that—bring black kids together."

"You mean a place to meet other *rich* black kids! I'm not like that, Ma. I don't care about what other kids' parents do for a living or how fancy their house is."

Ma smiled. "That's what I like about you," she said, kissing my forehead. "Anything special you want for dinner?"

"Chicken."

"Should have guessed."

In the car I took a deep breath and asked, "Why'd Clair call so early?"

"She called about her daughter. I don't know if you remember her. Rebecca?"

I shook my head.

"Well, I know you remember me telling you about Clair's nervous breakdown a few years back. . . ."

"Yeah, I remember that."

"Seems Clair's been having a hard time since then. First she and her husband split up. Then she lost her teaching position because she was taking so much time off since she wasn't well. Now, it seems, her oldest daughter,

Rebecca, is pregnant and Clair wants to know if she can come stay with us until the baby comes. She thinks Rebecca needs a quieter place. All of the other children put too much stress on her." Ma sighed, then frowned. "Seems like history repeating itself. First Clair getting pregnant before she had a chance to finish college. Now Rebecca . . ."

"Why can't Rebecca stay with her husband?"

"She's not married, Feni. She's fifteen."

"Fifteen? Ma, are you playing a joke on me or something?"

Ma pulled the car up in front of Roper Academy, but I didn't budge. "I would never joke about something like this, Feni," she said firmly.

We stared at each other for a moment, her eyes worried behind her glasses.

"I don't want a pregnant girl in our house, Ma," I said, trying to keep my voice even.

"Feni"—Ma reached to touch my face but I pulled away—"don't be judgmental. Give her a chance. . . ."

"I don't want her here!"

Ma put her hands on her lap. "I don't know if I'm going to say yes or what. I feel like I owe Clair. We were so tight at Spelman. Then we lost touch. I always swore I'd do anything for her. I still want to believe that."

"What about me?" I wasn't yelling, but my voice sounded too loud in the small car.

"We can talk about it all tonight. But I think it would be nice to have some company in the house. It's been such a

13

long time. We have all this space, and Bernadette could tutor Rebecca—"

"What's to talk about? I said I don't want a pregnant girl in our house!"

"And *I* said we'd talk later! This is about more than what *you* want for once, Afeni! If you can't understand what being close to somebody means and wanting to help them when they ask for help, then you have a lot of growing to do! You don't even know Rebecca, so how can you know whether or not you want her in our house?"

"Who's going to look after her?" I asked. "You? You work all the time, and Marion is not much better! I know it'll all fall on me. I'll be the one stuck in the house cleaning up after her. And I know she'll end up in my room, because I'm not about to let anyone stay in Grandma's room, and you'll say the guest room is too drafty. So I'll be the one who'll have to hear her crying herself to sleep at night because she misses her mommy! Not you, Ma! So don't tell me it's *our* decision because it's not! I don't care how tight you and Clair were at Spelman, our house isn't some home for pregnant girls! This is my life too, now, and I'm going to decide who I do and don't want in it!"

"Look, Feni," Ma said, "you're twelve today, not thirty. Now, when you're old enough to be taking care of me, you can tell me what to do."

"I never had to take care of you?" I asked, cocking an eyebrow in her direction.

Ma swallowed and gripped the steering wheel with both hands. Before the words were out, I regretted it. "I'm sorry.

I don't mean to throw it in your face all the time," I nearly whispered.

"Well, it's in my face, Feni. Again."

Gathering my books together, I took one last look at her before I climbed out of the car.

"Have a happy birthday today," she said, looking straight ahead as I turned to slam the door.

Two

Roper Academy was founded by Quakers and is private but not snobby private. We don't have to wear uniforms or remember the biography of some ancient-looking founder. And because it's in the middle of town, we aren't secluded from other kids who aren't students here. It starts at kindergarten and goes to twelfth grade, so we're all supposed to be super close by the time we graduate. Caesar is my only friend.

In the warm crowded halls, students clumped together like oatmeal, wearing wool and flannel. Each outfit looked like it took a lifetime to put together.

I stood against the wall, waiting for Caesar, watching kids stuff rubber boots into their bright red lockers and put on leather shoes. The girls were giggly. The boys passing walked with their shoulders thrown back, their eyes hooded. Some kids screamed out, "Hey, Feni," and "Happy birthday, Feni Beanie." A few kids looked at me and smiled. I smiled back and tried not to look inviting.

"You think too much," Bernadette says to me sometimes. "You're like me in that way," she adds, smiling. She was my teacher in the fifth grade. She and Marion have been together for a long time. Now they're like aunts to me. Sometimes Bernadette and I stare at each other for a long time without saying anything. And when Ma or Marion asks us why we stare like that, Bernadette smirks, saying, "We're the same person somewhere inside. We have souls that are small, dark, and quiet as nuns."

At the sound of the first bell, groups scurried like birds and disappeared behind dark wooden doors. I stood at my locker and took out the picture of Grandma. She looked up at me and smiled.

"Afeni," Caesar called, standing at the classroom door, "I've been waiting for you in the classroom."

"We're supposed to meet by the lockers," I yelled down the hall, just as the late bell rang.

Caesar crossed her eyes at me. "Birthday pinch," she whispered, pinching my arm as I slid past her.

"Have to tell you something. You're going to die!" I said.

"What?" Caesar whispered. "Tell me now."

"Later," I mouthed, taking my seat.

In class Caesar passed me a note that said, *Happy Birthday, Feni. Write me a note and tell me what you have to tell me.* There was a stick of Doublemint gum wrapped in the paper.

I took the gum out and wrote at the bottom of the paper, *Later. It's too much to tell in one note. Thanks for the gum.*

When Caesar read the note, she turned around, raised her eyebrows, and rubbed her hands together.

"Turn to page fifty-one in *Our World,*" Ms. Temple, our

history teacher, said. Books slammed onto desks. Pages flipped noisily. On page fifty-one a pilgrim gave a Native American a turkey. They smiled at each other. The drawing was done in watercolors and the Native American had soft, sad eyes.

When Ms. Temple began reading out loud, Caesar turned to me and crossed her eyes. We both knew that pilgrims had given Native Americans blankets with smallpox on them. Caesar is part Native American and part black. We knew not to call Native Americans "Indians." Ms. Temple read and we didn't listen. In history we knew to hold on to what Ms. Temple said only until we were tested. After that we threw it away.

I doodled in the margin of my notebook, drawing blankets with little dots on them and Native Americans dying. My stomach dipped when I remembered Rebecca coming to our house.

The wind whistled past the windows. Ms. Temple said, "Do the questions at the end of the chapter, quietly. I'll collect your work and mark it as a quiz." The class groaned. In front of me a note was passed. Someone giggled and Ms. Temple looked up. Soon after I finished my quiz, the bell rang.

"Someone is coming," I said to Caesar after class. We were standing in front of my locker, watching the halls fill up again.

"Who?" Caesar asked excitedly. Her hair was pulled back away from her face like mine. It was black and brown and had blue dye in the front.

18

"I can't believe your mother let you put that stuff in your hair," I said, reaching out to touch the streak of blue.

"She didn't. I put it on in the girls' bathroom this morning. I'm gonna wash it out before I get home."

"It looks cool."

"Who's coming?" Caesar asked again.

"I don't know," I said. "A girl. Her name's Rebecca." Suddenly, Rebecca's face came to me clearly. A long time ago, when we were living in an apartment waiting for our house to get built, Clair and her kids visited us. The kids tore through the apartment, knocking over things, breaking my toys. The oldest was Rebecca. She had evil gray eyes and yelled at the little kids. They listened to her for a while, then tore through the house some more. Rebecca watched the television. She asked me if there were old movies on. I was seven then and didn't watch movies. Rebecca looked in our refrigerator when she thought no one was watching. She touched our stuff and frowned.

I told all this to Caesar and her eyes opened wide.

"Why is she coming?" Caesar asked.

I shrugged. For some reason this was the part I wanted to keep to myself for a while. "Me, Ma, and Marion are going to talk about it tonight. Maybe later you can come over. For cake and stuff."

Even before she shook her head no, I knew what the answer would be. "I can't," she said. Then she looked at me. "I'm sorry."

"That's okay," I said, feeling my stomach close up. "She's not drinking anymore."

Caesar nodded. "I know. It's just kind of hard."

A long time ago, drunk, Ma had said some not-so-nice things to Caesar, and Caesar had left the house. She had not been back since.

"She hasn't drunk in a long time."

"That's good. I'm real glad she stopped."

"You think you'll come over soon?" I asked, fidgeting with my notebook so I wouldn't have to see her say "no."

Caesar reached out and touched my shoulder. "Yeah," she said.

When I looked up, she was smiling.

We held hands walking down the hall and went in different directions at the stairway.

Halfway up the stairs, Caesar stopped. "You going to Jack and Jill tonight?"

"Caesar, I hate Jack and Jill."

"I know, but they'll probably have a party for you."

"You know what I hate more than Jack and Jill?" I asked.

"A Jack and Jill party." Caesar laughed and headed toward her class.

In study hall, which is actually the giant auditorium, we were supposed to sit and read. But I could not stop thinking about Rebecca. I could not stop wondering about how she'd gotten pregnant.

I pulled out the silver frame and stared at Grandma. Her eyes followed me. They wanted to know more about Rebecca too. They wanted to know why.

Three

MARION HAD BEEN A PROSECUTOR FOR FIVE YEARS
when she walked into her office one day and quit. The
next day she stopped drinking. A week later she got a job
as a legal-aid attorney, defending poor people who couldn't
afford to hire lawyers. The night she won her first case we
had the biggest party in Seton.

Marion arrived for my birthday dinner at eight o'clock
wearing blue jeans and a sweater. When I came downstairs,
she held me away from her, turned me from side to side,
and shook her head. "I knew you when you were just a
thought," she said, and pulled my present from her bag.
"Go on and open it," she said. "It's from me and
Bernadette."

"Where is Bernadette, anyway?" I asked, tearing into
the present.

"She has her support group tonight. Gay and lesbian
teachers. They talk about how hard it is to teach in such a
straight environment. It's good for her."

"How come you don't go to a gay-and-lesbian lawyers
support group?" I asked.

"Because all the legal-aid lawyers I work with *are* gay!" Marion laughed.

Marion and Bernadette have been together for eight years. They met at a professional women's conference in New York. Two years later Bernadette moved here and they bought a house together two miles away from us. It's a happily-ever-after story, I guess.

Marion's the only daughter of a white mother and black father. She could be white but says she isn't. Her skin is the color of sand, and her gray eyes have flecks of gold in them.

"You like that, Feni?"

I was staring down at the jeans and sweater Marion had bought me.

"It's the greatest. I'm wearing this tomorrow." I kissed her on the cheek.

"I was going to get you some shoes, but I didn't know what size you wear." Marion sat on the couch, pulled an ashtray across the coffee table, and lit a cigarette. "You're growing so fast," she said, exhaling a stream of smoke. "Makes me feel old."

Ma came out of the kitchen carrying a plate of chicken with white sauce. She had been experimenting with French dishes.

"Feni, that's excellent. I love that sweater. Marion, you shouldn't have . . . ," Ma exclaimed.

"Yes, she should have," I cut in. "It's my birthday!"

"You're right, Feni," Marion said. "Birthdays are meant to be celebrated!"

Marion looked at me. "Go try them on," she said as I

headed toward the den. "Don't take the tags off before we know if they fit. Those stores give you such a hard time if you don't have the tags."

"I know what you mean," Ma said. "Don't get anything on them, Feni!"

"You know what Clair had the nerve to say to me today?" Marion asked Ma. "I tell you, she says she's better since the breakdown, but I think that woman is still halfway out of her mind. Sometimes I don't know what to think."

"What'd she say?"

I came out of the den zipping up the jeans.

"Look at *you*!" Marion said, stubbing out her cigarette. "Isn't she something, Catherine? Turn around and let us get a better look."

I turned slowly.

Ma smiled. "Perfect! Just perfect!" She picked up her camera. "Stand close to Marion, Feni . . . and smile."

Ma clicked four more pictures before she let me take the outfit off.

"Come sit over at the table, Marion. Hurry up and get changed, Feni, before this food gets cold."

"Now," Marion said, when I came back into the dining room, "about Clair and Rebecca! Since Peter left—"

"Who's Peter?" I asked, sitting down at the table and helping myself to some chicken. "And why does Rebecca have to stay here anyway?"

"Let her finish, Feni," Ma said. "Peter was Clair's husband. I knew that no-good man wouldn't be around long."

"Well, they were together nearly sixteen years," Marion

23

said. She turned to me. "I know your mother told you it was the three of us everywhere at Spelman—me, Catherine, and Clair. You would never see one of us without the other two." Marion bit into her chicken and spooned some green beans onto her plate. "This is delicious. Give me the recipe before I leave."

"Then what happened?" I interrupted.

"Well," Marion said, "they had six children. Clair was a teacher. But when Peter left, everything fell apart."

"Last time Clair and I talked," Ma said softly, "I was still drinking. I should have called her a long time ago. It's been too much time between. It'd be nice to see her again."

"I think Rebecca in this house will close that gap a little bit. If that girl is anything like Clair, she must have a little bit of the devil in her."

"Oh, great!" I said. "Just bring the devil right into the house. Don't mind me!"

"I think you two just might get along," Marion said, cocking an eyebrow.

"I doubt it very seriously."

"She'll need all kinds of things, Marion—a tutor—"

"Bernadette could tutor her. She already said she would."

Ma was silent for a moment. "She'll need clothes, a doctor, childbirth classes. But most of all, attention."

Marion laughed. "Between all of us that girl will have too much of all of those things."

"Count me out!" I said. "But then again, I guess it doesn't matter what *I* say, since you two have it all figured out."

Ma and Marion exchanged looks.

"You know it matters, Feni," Marion said.

"How come she can't stay with you?" I asked her. "You and Bernadette have a big house."

"Clair doesn't think I live the right kind of life," Marion said.

I picked up my fork again and mumbled, "That's so stupid."

"Clair doesn't understand about me and Bernadette. She doesn't understand how happy we are together, how that's what matters," Marion said. "I can't make her."

The dining room grew silent. Ma chewed her chicken slowly, and Marion moved the beans around on her plate. I wanted to tell Marion I loved her. And how much I liked Bernadette, that Bernadette was one of Roper's best teachers and I didn't care how they lived.

"How long does she have to stay here?" I asked. The idea of what was happening was starting to sink in.

"Until the baby comes, at least," Ma said.

I pushed my plate away from me.

"Feni . . . ," Ma began.

"Feni, nothing!" I yelled, ramming my chair back. "This is an awful thing to give me for my birthday!" Marion reached out to touch me, but I moved away.

"What if I don't want anybody in this house with us?" I asked, not caring that Marion looked surprised.

"Then," Ma said calmly, "I guess you'll have to get over it, because she's coming."

"Why wouldn't you want her here, Feni?" Marion

asked. "I would think it would be nice to have some company."

"Then you take her," I said.

"That's enough," Ma said. Marion pushed her plate away and lit another cigarette.

"She'll need company," Marion said calmly. "I work most of the day, and so does your mother."

I folded my arms and looked away. Something in Marion's voice reminded me of the power grown-ups have over me and how easy it is for them to do what they want with my life.

"Whatever," I said.

"I think it'll be good for you," Ma said.

"No, it won't. It'll be good for *you* and Marion. You're the ones feeling all guilty about Clair."

I left the table without excusing myself and went upstairs.

Downstairs I heard Marion say, "She's something else, isn't she?" and Ma say, "She's her father's daughter, all right."

I opened Grandma's frame and stared at her. She was still smiling.

Four

LATER THAT NIGHT, LONG AFTER MARION HAD LEFT, MA tapped on my door and peeked in.

"I guess you don't want any cake," she said.

"I guess I don't."

"It's from Ms. Maxie's bakery. Buttercream frosting."

"I said I don't want any."

She came in and sat on the side of my bed.

"Feni . . . ," Ma began.

"Why does she have to come here? Why do you always have to ruin my birthday?"

I glared at Ma.

"How do I 'always ruin your birthday,' Feni?"

"There's always something happening. First you stopped drinking and it had to be on my birthday."

"Aren't you happy I stopped?"

"I'm happy *now,* but before, all I wanted you to do was drink something so you'd stop shaking and being crabby and tearing up paper all over the place. I hated that birthday. And you and Dad had to go and break up."

"That was after your birthday."

"That's only because you all didn't want to do it right *on* my birthday, but I knew he was leaving, and you weren't even speaking to each other. For all it mattered, he might as well have been gone already."

"Listen. Clair and I were close—always there for each other. And a tightness like that doesn't go away. Now she's having her troubles—"

"You're always saying I have to understand something. Well, I don't! I don't understand why that girl has to come here. I don't understand why she can't stay with Marion." I was yelling now and didn't care. Ma sat with her back straight at the other end of the bed and stared at me.

"Clair and Marion and I were close," Ma began again. She looked out the window like she was thinking about something far away from here. Her head tilted slightly, her hands still. "Back then it seemed like nothing could ever come between us."

"I've heard those stories a hundred times."

"You haven't heard everything, Feni. You'll never know everything that happened between us."

"The stuff I don't know about, I don't care about."

Ma continued as though she hadn't heard me. "When Clair got pregnant, she tried to hide it from everyone. But we were too close for secrets." Ma looked down at her hands, her voice dropping. "I think it hurt Marion the most. Marion had these big dreams for all of us. We were all going to live in Seton. Be neighbors. Then, it seemed like everything started happening at once. Clair left and Marion came out. We started growing apart. Marion had her women and I had my men."

"You think that's wrong?"

Ma shook her head. "No. I think a long time ago I did. Before Marion came out, I used to think that two people of the same sex together wasn't right. Back then I didn't know that there were so many ways people loved each other." Ma looked at me. "When I met Marion, she was a radical feminist out to save the whales and the world and anything else that might have needed saving at the time. I saw her power and her drive. Then I got to know her and knew that my mind had been closed for so long! I *did* have a hard time with it at first. I mean, I didn't know anything about lesbians and I was scared of them!" Ma smiled. "But Marion and I had been friends. Nothing had changed, really. Clair had the hardest time with it. She wasn't there when Marion was struggling. Clair still has a hard time. She doesn't really understand that it's not up to us to decide how people live."

"Other people decide how *I* live."

"They won't when you're grown," Ma said.

"That's not true. You said so yourself. There's always going to be someone deciding what I can and can't do. If it's not because I'm a kid, it'll be because I'm a woman. If it's not because I'm a woman, it'll be because I'm black."

Ma stared at me, surprised for a moment. Then something like fear took over the surprise. "Don't ever feel like you don't have power, Feni."

"I don't have the power to keep that girl from coming—"

"Her name is *Rebecca*. No more 'that girl.' Understand?"

"Yeah."

"You don't have to be her friend. But she is going to stay with us."

29

"I guess she can't sleep in the guest room?"

Ma shook her head. "It's way too cold in there for anybody this time of year."

"I *knew* it!" I said, folding my arms. "And now comes the part about Grandma's room. . . ."

"I was thinking that would be a good place for her. It's warm and near the bathroom."

"It's out of the question," I said firmly.

"What do you mean, 'It's out of the question'?"

"Not Grandma's room, Ma."

Ma touched my cheek and instantly, water welled up in my eyes. "Feni . . ."

"Don't do this to me, Ma. Don't give her Grandma's room."

"You have to start letting go, Feni."

"Don't make me, Ma," I cried. "Don't make me. Not now. Please not yet, Ma."

Five

MA WAITED UNTIL SHE THOUGHT I HAD CRIED MYSELF
to sleep before she left. When I heard her go downstairs
and close the den door, I tiptoed down the hall to
Grandma's room and pushed the door open. It was bare
now except for a double bed against the window and a
wooden rocking chair. Ma had taken down the pictures on
the wall years ago. Some of them were in the photo al-
bums downstairs. Dad had taken some.

"When you die," I whispered into the emptiness, "the
pieces of you get all separated."

Sitting on Grandma's bed, I cracked open the window.

My grandmother had been my best friend. I was eight
when she was dragged four blocks by a city bus while visiting San Francisco.

Grandma's friend Reese had been traveling with her and
said the bus driver didn't see Grandma step off the curb
and came around the corner of Market Street without
stopping. Grandma's dress sleeve got caught on the front
fender, and it was one of the dresses Grandma had made
herself, so it was double-stitched at every seam.

When Grandma died, I didn't speak for two months. There was a fire in my head threatening to burn me alive. But I sat by my window, letting the hot summer sun burn it to ashes.

They buried her beside my grandfather, whom I never knew, in a small plot that said CALEB.

"A long time ago," Grandma had said, when we visited my grandfather and put white lilies on his grave, "colored folks weren't allowed to be buried here. Your granddaddy is probably rolling over and over, knowing that he is buried in Shepherd Cemetery. Lord, I can just see him smiling from ear to ear." Grandma grinned then, at some little secret she and Grandpa shared. When she sat me down beside her husband's grave, her face grew calm. The silence of the graveyard scared me. Shivering, I moved closer to her.

"The day your granddaddy died, me and your mama had just come back from her checkup at the hospital. She was pregnant with you, and she was staying with us then, since she and Bernard had decided she needed some country air. So when we got back, I made her a nice bed, told her to climb in it, and went to tell your granddaddy that everything was fine. I walked as slow as I could over to where he was working, because I had this feeling in the back of my throat like something wasn't right somewhere. When I got there, couldn't have been more than a hundred feet from the house, your granddaddy still had the pinking shears in his hands. He was sitting against that tree like he was waiting for me. Had his eyes wide open and sweat dripping down his pretty brown face."

32

Grandma looked around the graveyard. "Now, the birds had been making noise all morning, but when I got to where your granddaddy was sitting, everything became as quiet as it is now." Grandma picked up one of the lilies and held it to my nose. I inhaled and it tickled my nostrils. "I took a quarter from my apron pocket and closed your granddaddy's eyes."

We were silent for a long time. I stared at the dark gray stone, wishing I had known the man who lay beneath it. RANDALL CALEB, the stone said, 1919–1989. MAY HE REST IN PEACE. Underneath that was a poem, engraved in tiny letters. I had memorized it a long time ago:

> Your world is as big as you make it.
> I know for I used to abide
> in the narrowest nest in a corner,
> my wings pressing close to my side
> but I sighted a distant horizon
> where the skyline encircled the sea
> and I throbbed with a burning desire
> to travel this immensity
> I battled the cordons around me
> and cradled my wings on the breeze
> then soared to the uttermost reaches
> with rapture, with vigor, with ease!

As I read the poem silently, I felt Grandma watching me. When I'd finished, I looked at her and waited.

"Your mother and father are good people, Feni. They love you very much."

I nodded. Grandma continued and it seemed almost as if she were talking to someone else—someone miles and miles away.

"Women are strong, Feni. Survivors. The Bible says we were made from the rib of Adam, but that may not be true."

"But Grandma," I interrupted, "you said the Bible is Truth!"

"Yeah. Yeah. I know what I said, sweetheart. That was a long time ago."

"Before you stopped going to church, Grandma?"

She nodded. "Long before I stopped going to church."

"But why did you stop going?"

"I stopped going because I didn't believe anymore, Feni. Can you understand that?"

I nodded. "It's like when I didn't believe in Santa anymore."

Grandma smiled. "Exactly. I stopped believing in waiting, Afeni. If something is going to happen to me after I die, then it will. No use worrying and praying while I still have plenty of this life to live. It's easier this way. But that's not what I'm trying to tell you. What I want to say is that in this world, there are all types of women. Some of us make mistakes and some of us seem weak sometimes and others seem full of strength. Some don't want to bear children, others can't. Some women marry once, or eight and nine times, and others never do."

"Like Marion?"

A frown flickered across Grandma's face. She didn't like Marion. "Sometimes. But we're not talking about Marion, sweetheart. We're talking about your mother. She's a

34

strong woman. She makes mistakes sometimes. Sometimes it seems like she doesn't love you, but I want to tell you this—"

"Sometimes it seems like Ma doesn't care about me."

"But she does, Feni. That's my point. Your mother, she has a big problem now. A very big one. And she's going to have to get through it on her own. You have to bear with her, Feni. Don't be stubborn. Don't be angry."

"But sometimes she makes me so mad, Grandma. When she drinks . . ."

"That liquor makes your mama weak."

"And it makes Dad mad. Then they fight. They fight so much."

Grandma looked down at me. "People come together sometimes and it isn't a bit more meant to be than I don't know what. It just doesn't make sense to anybody."

"Like Ma and Dad. I don't think they love each other. And when Ma drinks, I get scared."

"Someday your mama's going to realize that drinking doesn't heal any wounds," Grandma said softly. "I look at her and I see she's all broken up inside. She wants something she isn't getting."

"What does she want?"

Grandma squeezed my hand and pulled me to my feet. "She's the only one who knows, Feni." Her voice was soft and rich against the quiet. Together we made our way past the silent tombstones, toward home.

Walking back from my grandmother's funeral in the white dress I vowed never to wear again, I was silent. Ma

35

and my father walked far apart from each other. I stopped a little away from where the car waited for us and turned toward the grave.

"Are you okay?" Ma asked, bending down to wipe my eyes. "Blow," she said, holding a white handkerchief firmly to my nose.

Hundreds of people were around us. The women patted Ma and stared sadly down at me. All of them wore black. Only Ma looked strong.

Now, leaning back against the firm pillows, I sighed. Grandma had been dead a long time. Soon, I knew, I'd have to begin to let go.

Six

NEAR DAWN I MADE MY WAY TO MA'S ROOM AND climbed into bed beside her. Sleepily, she reached over to hug me and slowly realized I was there.

"Did you have a bad dream?" she asked groggily.

"I dreamed about Rebecca. I dreamed she was having the baby in the house and nobody was home but me. I was scared, Ma."

Ma pulled me closer to her. "Are you worried, Feni?"

I nodded into the darkness. "I'm scared to have a pregnant girl here. She's only three years older than me!"

"I know, sweetheart," Ma said, her voice growing clearer. "I wanted to talk to you about that tonight, but we got so lost in everything else."

"You wanted to talk about Rebecca's baby?"

"Uh-uh. I wanted to talk about boys and love and getting pregnant so young."

I felt my face grow hot. "I don't even have a boyfriend."

"Thank God you don't. I'd have to go upside his head with a frying pan!"

"Boys are so dumb sometimes."

"I'm glad you still think that way."

"But Ma . . . ?"

"Hmmm . . . ?"

"Why do you think that happened to Rebecca? I mean, she's so young and everything."

Ma groaned into sitting position. "It scares me a little how much Rebecca's life is following Clair's. It's not exactly the same, Clair having some college behind her and all, but I'm sure Rebecca didn't want this to happen. I don't know Rebecca anymore. The Rebecca I knew was small and shy."

"The one I remember was mean and bossy. You sure we're talking about the same person?"

Ma laughed. "I'm sure."

"You think Rebecca and her boyfriend love each other?"

Ma thought for a moment. "I think sometimes girls are looking for love when they get pregnant. They need love or maybe they want something real to love. And at the time a baby seems to be the perfect thing. I hope you never feel that way, Feni."

"Does it just happen, Ma? Do you wake up one day and feel like there's not enough love in your life and then you go out and find a boyfriend and—"

"Sex is a lot more serious than that, Feni. There's love first. Then you start feeling like you'll burst if you can't kiss the person. Then you want to touch each other. Then you want sex. But love should come way before that."

"What if you just *think* you love the person?"

Ma pulled me closer to her and brushed the hair away from my face. "You have to be sure. You have to really know the person you're with. I mean, with AIDS and everything else going around, you have to be able to talk to your lover about their past. About their sex life. It's hard to have a conversation like that with someone you just *think* you love. But don't worry," she said, giving me a shake. "You'll know when you're sure."

"It all seems like it's way in the future, Ma. Like I'm watching it on a big-screen TV and it doesn't have anything to do with me."

"That's the perfect place for it," Ma said. "Way in the future!"

"You think Clair still loves Rebecca?"

"Of course. It takes a lot for a mother to stop loving her child, Feni."

"You think Marion's mother still loves her?"

"I'm sure of it."

"Before this Rebecca thing I didn't even think about sex. Now I'm thinking about it all the time."

"Well, don't think too hard," Ma said.

"Everything's about sex, though. Rebecca . . . Marion . . ."

"Well, I can't really speak for Rebecca, because I don't know her. But as for Marion and Bernadette, their relationship is about love, Feni. Marion and Bernadette love each other."

Ma lay back down beside me. "When it's about love first, that's the best way. That's the way you remember it way into old age."

"It's so confusing. I mean, I don't like boys so much now. Does that mean I won't ever like them?"

"Time tells, Feni. And if you don't, that's okay too."

"Would you still love me if I grew up to be gay?"

"Of course."

"Would you still love me if I came home pregnant like Rebecca?"

"Of course, but that doesn't have to happen. When you think you're ready for sex, we can talk about safer sex and birth control. I'll even take you to the clinic. But I hope you'll wait a few years before you fall in love that way. I want you to go to college, Feni, and do well. You'll have so much time for babies."

"But would you still *love* me?"

"Yes, I would still love you."

"What if I came home with a baby *and* a girlfriend!"

"Feni . . . !"

"Just checking, Ma!"

"Just let's talk before any kind of sex happens, okay?"

I climbed farther under the covers and smiled. "Okay."

Ma closed her eyes.

"Is she fat or skinny?"

"I haven't seen her in years."

"You think she's taller than me?"

"I doubt it. You're pretty tall."

"Her eyes were gray. I remember that. Remember, Grandma said gray-eyed people were evil."

"Your grandma was full of ideas about people."

"She was the greatest."

"Um-hmm."

"Ma?"

"Hmmm . . . ?"

"You think Grandma would have liked Rebecca staying here?"

"She would have thought it was *different*."

I laughed. "Grandma would be mad. She'd say"—I lowered my voice and spoke slowly—" 'Now Catherine, 'taint right! Just 'taint right, you raisin' my Feni around girls in trouble.' Isn't that what she would've said?"

"You have her down, all right."

"She was the greatest."

The house creaked in the silence. Ma's breath became steady against my arm.

"Ma . . . ?"

"Fey, do you know what time it is?" Ma asked sleepily.

"Time to say I love you." I turned on my side. "Good night."

Ma laughed sleepily, pulled me closer to her, and sighed.

Seven

ON SUNDAY, MA LEFT EARLY TO MEET REBECCA AT THE airport, and I stayed behind to shovel the slush out of the driveway.

As I shoveled the last of the snow into a small gray pile, the sun came out. Shielding my eyes, I looked out over the street. Seton is a small black Pennsylvanian suburb surrounded by mountains. The Victorian houses stand far apart from each other, and the people who live in them are doctors and lawyers and bankers. A lot of families have kids who get sent away to private schools in the fall. Looking out over the quiet street made me sad all of a sudden. I wondered how many Rebeccas had been sent from here while the rest of us, the "nice kids," were being sent to Jack and Jill, White Gloves and Manners, and dance school—all the places nice kids go to meet other "nice kids."

Upstairs in my room, I touched the clean blue sheets we had put on Rebecca's bed. For a moment I felt like we were cheating her, her small roll-away cot looking dwarfed beside my double bed. The thin mattress smelled like the attic. But there was no way I was going to let her or anyone else stay in Grandma's room. Even if it meant sharing my bedroom with a pregnant girl.

Although the house was spotless, I decided to vacuum the living room. The center of our living room sinks down into a small carpeted area with a fireplace opposite the large fish tank.

By the time I'd finished, Ma's car was pulling up. Ma had left a roast in the microwave, and I pressed it for ten on my way to the door.

"Hi, honey. Get the other bag out of the car, please," Ma said, bustling in with a bag of groceries. "We stopped at the store. Rebecca doesn't eat meat."

I held the door for her, then went to the trunk. I couldn't see anyone on the passenger side until the girl lifted her head from the backseat.

She groaned as she got out of the car. The first thing I saw was her stomach beneath a too-small coat. I was peeking from around the trunk and she turned and caught me.

"You never seen a pregnant girl before?" She pulled her lips into a thin line and the dimples on the side of her face deepened. There were pimples dotting her forehead, and above them, curly hair cut short like a boy's. I glanced away quickly.

"Well, have you?" She came around to the back of the car and watched as I lifted the groceries out. "Man, this sure is the country," she said, taking a look around. "Nobody told me I was going to the country."

I held the bag of groceries in one hand and slammed the trunk door with the other.

43

Rebecca pulled a small suitcase from the backseat, then followed me inside.

"Wow!" she said, looking around the living room. "This is like a mansion or something." I must have frowned a little. "You people are rich. I didn't know rich black people existed except on television." She put her bag down and walked over to the fish tank. She was a little clumsy because she leaned forward slightly to hide her stomach. "Look at this!" she said. "Look at all those fishes."

"Fish."

She straightened up and turned to me. "Look. Just 'cause I'm in your ritzy little house," she hissed, "doesn't mean you gonna teach me how to talk and tell me what to do. I don't want to be in this mansion in the boring country nohow! You think you special or something, but I know all about you, Feni Harris. Your mama says you don't talk to nobody and you don't have any friends. So you better consider yourself lucky that I'm here, whether I'm here saying *fishes, fish,* or *fried fish*!" She put her hands on her hips and stared at me.

"The word's still *fish*," I said, taking the groceries into the kitchen.

"I guess we should try to refreeze this," Ma said, standing at the microwave holding the roast in her hands. "Rebecca's a vegetarian, so we won't be eating it for a while."

I began putting the groceries away. "I still eat meat. Just because she doesn't, does that mean everybody's diet has to change?"

44

Ma looked at me. "I still eat meat too. We'll work around that." She put the meat in the refrigerator, then came over to me and looked out the window above my head. "I wonder where Marion is. I'm sure she didn't forget about today," she said. "Rebecca seems like a sweet girl, doesn't she?"

I was about to say something, but Rebecca came into the kitchen. "Ms. Harris, this is a great house!" She sat down heavily and rubbed her stomach. "It must have cost you a million dollars. That couch is real leather, isn't it? I saw a couch like that once in Seaman's. It cost two thousand dollars. I told my boyfriend that's the couch I want when we get married. Only, the one I'm getting is beige, not brown. But I like your brown one a lot. Is that where I'm going to be sleeping? I need a nap."

"No," Ma said, smiling. "We moved an extra bed into Feni's room. I thought it would be nice if you two were together." A frown crossed Rebecca's face, but then she smiled quickly. "Why don't you take a nap while we get dinner ready? You say all I have to do is steam this tofu awhile and pour some barbecue sauce over it?"

Rebecca nodded and I looked at the cheesy-looking white lump Ma was holding. "What's that?"

"It's tofu." Rebecca smirked. "Really good protein. You gonna show me to my room?" She got up slowly and exhaled. "I never thought getting up would be so hard."

I looked at Ma, but she was reading the back of the tofu package and frowning.

Eight

"LOOK AT ALL THESE DOLLS!" REBECCA SQUEALED, darting clumsily to the shelves beside my bed. "There must be a hundred of them!"

"Seventy-four," I mumbled. The dolls were lined up in size order on three shelves.

"I used to have dolls like this," Rebecca said. "I used to have a hundred dolls. They were from all over the world, every color, every size. I had more dolls than any girl in the world." She reached for one, then stopped. "Can I touch them? Or are you selfish?"

"No, you cannot," I said.

But she pulled a brown baby doll wrapped in a blue blanket from the shelf anyway. "Oh, he's beautiful," she said, cuddling the doll to her chest. "Bless him." Her voice changed and she turned to me. "I had a doll like him too. I had all kinds of dolls!"

"What happened to them?" I was sitting on the side of my bed, and it was hard to take my eyes off her stomach.

"I don't know. They all got gone. Some went here. Some went there. I gave a lot of them to charity. I'm generous by nature. Least that what people tell me." She took the doll over to the cot. "This is my bed, right?" There was a whisper of disappointment in her voice as she laid the doll down and opened her bag.

"I didn't bring my best stuff . . . ," she said, looking up at me. "I always pack lightly when I go on trips. I've been all kinds of places."

I stared at the pitiful bundle of clothes she took from the suitcase. There were two or three dingy-looking pairs of underwear, a white sweatshirt, and a pair of jeans that had been cut out in the front and restitched with elastic. There was a light blue pair of stretch-material pants like the old lady kind my grandmother hated and a flowered bathrobe with a frayed ribbon where a belt should be.

"I think I forgot my pajamas, but I can sleep in a T-shirt or something."

She looked at me for what seemed like a long time until I finally got embarrassed and looked away. "Do you always stare like that? Because if you do, you're rude," she said.

I played with the edge of my bedspread and said nothing. I hated Rebecca.

"Anyway, what goes on in your mind when you sit there staring like you want something from me? You got all this stuff. What more do you want?"

"What do you mean, what more do I want?" I said, tightening my hands into fists. "I don't want anything from anybody. Least of all you. What can you give me? You don't have anything."

"Oh, don't go losing your mind. You're a brat. That's what you are. You sure could use a kick in the butt."

"You sure aren't going to give it to me," I said weakly. What right did she have, coming into my house and thinking she could take over?

"I wouldn't waste my time, selfish-head. You got all these dolls and still you want more stuff."

"I don't play with those dolls anymore. I'm too big for them."

Rebecca held the shirt she was folding in midair. "Get outta here. You're what? Eleven? Twelve?"

"I'm too old," I said again.

"That's too bad. I played with my dolls until I was fourteen. And I'm completely in love with him," she said, gesturing toward the doll again. "I don't care what people say. When I played with my dolls, I forgot everything. Nothing mattered. Nothing. Nothing was real except the stuff I made up with my dolls. I talked to them and everything. They talked back to me too."

"I had talking dolls once."

"Mines wasn't no talking dolls. Mines was the kind like those. They didn't really talk. Only, they talked to me sometime."

You're a little bit crazy, I wanted to say. But Rebecca's eyes were clouded over and her voice had dropped to a whisper. So I leaned a little closer to hear.

"They used to tell me the way things was. My moms, she's not so well, you know. She acts strange sometimes still. I would go in the room and me and my dolls would find a place and just talk about it. I have all these brothers and sisters, and they drive me crazy. The house is always full of screaming and fighting and everything. So me and my dolls would find a quiet place like in the closet or somewhere and we'd just talk."

"What'd your dolls say?" I asked, inching toward the door.

Rebecca's voice became normal again. "What do you think they said?"

I shrugged and she moved her suitcase and lay back on the bed.

"What'd your dolls say when you stopped playing with them? Did they say, 'Feni, you not playing with us no more 'cause your daddy went away'? Is that what they said?"

"I don't care about my father going away," I said, realizing I had not touched a doll since my dad left.

"Well, I stopped playing with those dolls when I got me a boyfriend, and that's when the dolls stopped talking." Rebecca took the baby doll in her arms and closed her eyes. "They just shut up and didn't say no more. It was something. It was like they never spoke," she said sleepily.

I stood in the doorway staring at her. She curled up with the doll, sighed, and turned away from me. When I heard the soft sound of her snoring, I stepped out of the room and slammed the door.

Nine

MARION CAME OVER IN TIME FOR DINNER, HER ARMS full of department-store bags. Rebecca and I were sitting silently across from each other at the kitchen table. We had not spoken since before her nap.

When Marion came into the kitchen, Rebecca's eyes slid across to me.

"She's a butch, right?" Rebecca whispered.

I wanted to slap her. "No, stupid! She's a lesbian."

"Same thing," she hissed. I balled my hands into fists, digging my nails into my palms. I had never punched a pregnant girl before. Actually, I had never punched anyone.

"Some lesbians don't like to be called butch. Just like some pregnant people don't like to be called *pregos*. Make any sense?"

Rebecca rolled her eyes at me but then flicked a look at Marion that showed my point had been made.

Marion was all smiles as she set bags in front of Rebecca. She kissed Rebecca on the forehead and Rebecca pulled away a little. "You grew up to be just beautiful, didn't you. Looks like Clair spit you right out of her mouth! Isn't she something, Catherine?" Ma was standing behind Marion

50

now, smiling. No one said anything. Rebecca blushed and stared down at the floor.

"Now, don't go getting jealous," Marion said to me as she tore into a bag. "I just bought a few things for Rebecca because I know she didn't have much time to shop before she left."

"That's where you've been all afternoon," Ma said, lifting the bags onto the table.

"You know," Marion said, "I haven't seen you since you were Feni's age. Maybe even a little younger. You probably don't even remember me."

"I remember you," Rebecca said. "Ma told me about you."

The kitchen grew silent.

"Did she?" Marion asked uneasily. "Well, what did she say?"

I was sitting opposite Rebecca with my chin in my hands. She didn't dare look anywhere but at the floor when she spoke. "She said you all were close at Spelman. Real close. How close were you to my ma?" She looked up then, and my eyes followed hers to Marion. We all waited.

"We were as tight as a braid," Marion said slowly. "All wound around each other like there was no beginning or end to us. Wasn't one of us any closer to the other than the next."

"But you're a dite, aren't you?"

"A what?" Marion asked, laughter in her eyes.

"A dite. That's what Ma says."

The laughter spilled over and Ma joined in. My eyes

51

met Rebecca's, and for a moment we were connected by our mutual confusion.

"The word is *dyke*," Marion said, wiping her eyes.

"Whatever the word is, that's what Ma says you are."

"What else does your mama say?" Marion asked. She was looking proudly down at Rebecca and didn't seem angry.

"Oh, she says all kinds of stuff. Ma's crazy sometimes. But when she talks about you all, mostly she talks about Spelman." Rebecca looked at Marion. "How come you're gay?" she asked out of the blue.

"That's rude," I said, and Rebecca cut her eyes at me.

"Nobody's talking to you!"

"Well, you two have certainly hit it off." Marion took a sweater from one of the bags and held it to Rebecca's shoulders.

"You think this'll fit?"

Rebecca's mouth dropped open when she looked at the sweater. "It's beautiful!" She stood slowly and held the sweater to her. "It's so soft." Part of the sweater sat on her stomach. "All these bags are stuff for me?"

"Nobody bought me anything," I mumbled, ripping up a piece of tissue.

"Help me set the table, Feni," Ma said.

In the dining room I could hear Rebecca oohing and aahing with each rip of paper. "That sure was rude of her to ask Marion about being gay," I whispered.

"That's the way you learn, isn't it? By asking?"

"If that was me, I would be on punishment for a week!"

"I don't know, Feni. Marion doesn't mind you asking questions."

"You mind?"

"Of course not."

"You used to before. Before you stopped drinking."

Ma put a salad fork down and looked at me. "My life is split in half, Feni—when I drank and when I stopped drinking. Everything I did when I drank, I'm sorry for. . . ."

"Whenever I think about that, I get mad."

"You should."

"Are you sorry for saying Rebecca could stay with us? I am."

"No, I'm not sorry, and I don't see why you are."

"She's rude, Ma. And she acts like she's not used to having nice stuff."

"She's not, Feni."

"Well, her family should get some nice stuff, then. At least that way, everybody could get used to it and not embarrass themselves when they come to somebody's house who has nice things!"

"They don't have the money, Feni."

"Then they should get some money."

"From where?" Ma asked too patiently.

"From wherever. . . ."

When Marion came out of the kitchen with Rebecca, Rebecca was wearing the sweater and a different pair of pants. It was not until Rebecca looked up at Ma to smile a thank-you that I realized: We were Rebecca's "wherever."

Ten

"I REALLY APPRECIATE YOU LETTING ME STAY HERE, MS. Harris," Rebecca said to Ma at dinner. "This house is lovely."

The words sounded as though they'd been rehearsed a thousand times. I grimaced, picking silently at my tofu. It tasted rubbery and bland beneath the mounds of barbecue sauce.

Ma and Marion took miniature bites and chewed them slowly. "I'm glad you're here," Ma said. "We could use some company in this empty house."

"How far is the doctor from here?" Rebecca asked.

Marion wiped her mouth and took a sip of water. "I found one who accepts Medicaid on Berkeley Street. She sounds like a nice woman. I made an appointment for Wednesday. I was hoping I could take you, or that Catherine would be able to, but my day is chock-full." She looked at Ma. "Yours isn't any better, is it?"

"Not Wednesday," Ma said. "I have meetings until four-thirty. Then, one of our members is celebrating ninety days' sobriety, so I want to be there."

A few years ago Ma and Marion stopped drinking and started going to Alcoholics Anonymous meetings. At the meetings other people who have stopped drinking help them get through "one day at a time." Ma gets scared sometimes and thinks that if things get too hard, she'll start drinking again. At the meetings people sit in a big circle and say, "My name is Joe S., and I'm an alcoholic." Then everyone says, "Hi, Joe," and Joe feels welcomed. Ma cried when she said the word *alcoholic* for the first time, she told me later. She had never called herself that before, and to her the word sounded like a curse.

"That's right," Marion said, stirring her tofu around in the barbecue sauce. "But Bernadette is free Wednesday. She could take you, Rebecca."

"Doesn't she have school?" I asked.

Marion shook her head. "She's taking Wednesday and Thursday off."

"When she was my teacher, she never took a day off."

"And you're all the better for it, Feni," Marion said, laughing.

"Is Bernadette my age?" Rebecca asked.

Ma and Marion exchanged looks and smiled. "She'd like to be," Marion said. "Bernadette's my girlfriend. We've been together more than eight years now."

"God, I'm surrounded," Rebecca mumbled. "Is that the only appointment you could get?"

"It's the earliest," Marion said. "Dr. Greenberg said she couldn't give us another until a couple of weeks from now, and with you being close to your last trimester and all,

Rebecca, we need to get you started on childbirth classes. Catherine and I will alternate as coaches."

Rebecca nodded and asked, "What's ninety days' sobriety?"

"Marion and I don't drink," Ma said, and she explained Alcoholics Anonymous to Rebecca.

"Any other questions? Like how much we weigh? Or when do we go to the bathroom?" I asked.

"That's enough, Feni," Ma said sharply.

Beneath the table Rebecca bumped against my leg hard.

I bumped her back and made the table shake. Ma and Marion looked at each other and said nothing.

"Clair mentioned that you're giving the baby up for adoption," Ma said. "Do you know the couple?"

"I'm gonna meet them. They're coming here sometime soon. All I know is that they can't have kids and they want a baby, so they're going to adopt mine. I wasn't going to let them at first. But me and Ma talked."

"Adoption is a good thing," Ma said. "I mean, if you're sure that's what you want."

Rebecca shrugged. "I don't know. Who cares, anyway? I could have more babies. I just hate the way people act about it. You'd think nobody in the world ever got pregnant when they was fifteen. My grandmother had her first baby when she was fifteen. And *her* grandmother was thirteen. People all the time staring and whispering behind my back. Like I care."

"People are going to judge you no matter what you do," Marion said. "Don't worry about other people. Worry about you."

Rebecca looked at her for a minute before she smiled. "You all think it's wrong, don't you? I mean, that I got pregnant."

Marion looked at Ma, then back at Rebecca. "Well, it's certainly not the *best* time, don't you think? With Clair sick and you still in high school. Later would have been a lot better."

"We're not here to judge, Rebecca," Ma said.

"Then how come you're here? How come you all are letting me stay here? Feni don't want me in her house."

"Don't put my name in it," I said.

"Well, you don't, do you?"

"You want me in *your* house?" I asked.

"Free country."

"We're here," Marion cut in, "because we have the things you need to get through this. There is space and quiet here, most times. And even though it doesn't seem like it with neither of us being able to go with you to the doctor on Wednesday, we do have time to spend with you and make sure you're all right."

"We're also here," Ma added, "because we want to make sure you keep up with your classes, finish school, and get a chance to make yourself into someone before starting a family. You're a bright girl, Rebecca. We don't want you to slip through the cracks. We won't have it."

"And," Marion continued, "we're here because we're Clair's friends."

"Friends don't do stuff like this for each other," Rebecca said.

Marion picked up a tiny piece of tofu. "These friends do," she said.

"I know this isn't a good time to be knocked up. I really do want to finish school and everything. . . ."

"You should have thought of that before," I said.

Rebecca glared at me, rolled her eyes, and stuck a chunk of tofu in her mouth.

We ate mostly in silence. Every now and then someone asked Rebecca a question about her mother or sisters and brothers. So, in pieces, I learned where Rebecca came from.

"What's Harlem like these days?" Marion asked at one point.

"The same," Rebecca said vaguely.

"I don't know Harlem anymore, so I have no idea what 'the same' is."

"The same raggedness. The same poor people. The same grayness. The same greatness. The same beautiful people," Rebecca mumbled.

"Do you miss it?" Ma asked.

"I've only been gone a day!"

"Don't get snotty," I said.

Rebecca sucked her teeth and turned to Marion. "The thing I know I'm gonna miss the most is all the stuff you see. Like once, I was walking down a Hundred Sixteenth Street. It was last fall when we was having all those hurricanes and it was gray and rainy a lot. But this one day it was just kind of cold and cloudy. I was coming back from buying Ma a pack of cigarettes—"

"Clair's smoking these days?" Ma asked.

"She's trying to quit. She started smoking because of her nerves," Rebecca said before continuing. "Anyway, there were these three kids and they were sitting on the stairs of this burned-out building. One of them had a Slinky—one of those green plastic ones—and he was trying to make it walk down the stairs like it does in the commercial. Only it wasn't doing it right. It would just go down one stair and stop. But the kid kept trying and his friends kept watching it."

"That trick never works for anybody," I said.

"But something about that . . . it just made me realize something," Rebecca said. "It just made me think that that's what everything's all about—things not working out the way they supposed to, the way somebody promised they would." She looked at Marion again. "It's always like that. Always the same."

Marion shook her head slowly. "I know what you mean," she said.

Ma was staring intently at Rebecca. "I look at you and see Clair all over again."

"But I'm not Clair. I'm *Rebecca*!" Rebecca said, without blinking.

"Do I know that!" Ma laughed, rising from the table. "I wish I could have dessert with you, but I want to try to make a meeting tonight." Ma carried her plate to the sink.

"I think I'll go with you, Catherine," Marion said, searching her bag for cigarettes. She put one in her mouth before rising.

"There's a cake in the freezer. If you put it in the microwave on three, it'll be room temperature."

At the doorway Ma said, "Make sure the kitchen is clean, Feni. I'll see you both later."

"I'll see you tomorrow night, maybe," Marion said, pulling on her coat before they disappeared out the door.

"Your moms is really pretty. She has that pretty skin. She probably never had a pimple." Rebecca ran her fingers lightly across her forehead. "Marion's nice too. I thought she'd be some big butch on a motorcycle or something."

"She has a motorcycle."

I got up and began piling the dishes into the dishwasher. Rebecca took one last bite of tofu, then pushed her dish toward me.

"They're nice and everything, but me, if I was going to be somebody's mother, I'd make a little time for dinner. They got up from this table like bats out of hell."

"They have careers and stuff. Ma works hard to make ends meet."

"You sound like a recording," Rebecca said. "And anyway, you guys are doing pretty well meeting ends. How many rooms in this house. Five? Six?"

"Well, she does have a career," I said.

"Well, she has a daughter too!"

I sprinkled some soap on the few dishes in the washer and closed the door. "That's none of your business, and besides, I don't mind. I like being by myself."

Rebecca leaned back. "She has to work on making tofu. It's really good when you know how to make it."

"I hate the way that stuff tastes."

"That's because you're not grown up enough. Tofu is for mature people like me. It's like wine. Maybe when you're older, you'll like it. Next time tell your mother to throw a hot dog in the microwave for you and just us ladies will eat the tofu."

"My mother doesn't like that junk either. Neither does Marion. They left most of it on their plates. It tastes like barbecued rubber bands."

Rebecca stared at the tablecloth.

"I'm sorry," I said quickly.

"For what? For not knowing nothing? You're just some rich kid way out here in the country. What do you know?"

"Seton isn't the country. It's the suburbs."

"Well, you don't learn nothing in the suburbs either. You stay stuck up in this mansion and don't talk to no-body. You just a little girl anyway. I don't care what you got to say."

"This isn't a mansion," I said, twisting the dish towel in my hands. "It's just a house. And it's my house and you're in it."

"Like I want to be. I hate this house. I hate Seton. And I hate you and your mother's nasty way of cooking tofu." She got up from the table and made her way slowly to the stairs. "I never wanted to come here. I wanted to stay where I was and have this baby. But my stupid mother thinks it's the nineteenth century and people shouldn't know I'm knocked up. Well, I am, so everybody better face the facts. And I'm not some street kid who has to be taken in by a rich family. I got my own family and my own friends, and I don't need to come all this way from home to bring some eleven- or twelve-year-old who doesn't know her neck from her elbow into reality!" She stomped up the stairs.

Eleven

THE ROOM WAS DARK AND QUIET WHEN I CAME UP-stairs. Rebecca looked too still to be sleeping, so I pulled the curtains open. Behind the trees the moon was full. I stared at it for a long time, liking the way the bare branches shot up through its whiteness.

"Don't even try talking to me about nothing, 'cause I don't feel like talking," Rebecca said hoarsely. She had been crying.

"I don't want to talk to you." I went over to my own bed and began to get undressed. "I just don't like you coming into my house thinking you can run things."

Rebecca turned onto her side. "I don't care about this house, Feni," she said softly. "I don't care about you or your mother or anything. If it was up to me, I'd be back in Manhattan with my sisters and brothers. I'd be back with my boyfriend and my friends. I have friends. I miss them too. They're gonna write me here. You just wait. I'm gonna be getting mail every day. My friends have lots of money to pay for stamps and envelopes and stuff. They have fancy cars and nice clothes."

"You always talk about money and all the stuff people have." I climbed under the covers and put my hands behind my head.

"That's what counts. That's what matters. The more money you have, the more power you have. You can do all kinds of things if you have a lot of money."

"Like what?"

"Like you don't know! Your family is loaded, so don't come asking me 'like what.' You can take trips to expensive places and buy houses and raise families. If you ain't got no money or you have to quit your job like my mother did when she got sick, you have to get money from the city to feed all of your babies, and then even after that some of your babies still be hungry. Plus, everybody likes you when you have money. Everybody wants to be your friend."

"Just because you have a lot of money doesn't mean you have a lot of friends."

"Well, maybe not you, 'cause you the type people don't want to go near. My friend Cloe was like you. She didn't hardly talk to nobody. She kept all of this stuff inside her all the time."

"What happened to her?"

"She got stupid and cracked out."

"She went crazy?"

Rebecca looked at me, letting her mouth drop open slightly. "Crack, Feni! C-r-a-c-k. Crack. It's little white rocks you buy in a vial and smoke. Hello?"

"I know what crack is. I just didn't know that's how you talked about somebody who was using it."

"Learn the language already," Rebecca said. "God! You're black. Talk like it."

"Kiss off!"

"Anyway," Rebecca continued, "Cloe lost it after that."

"How old was she?" I asked, not believing that someone young could do something that stupid.

"Fifteen like me. Only difference between me and Cloe is that she got stupid to get rid of those demons in her head. Real stupid."

"Well, I don't have any demons in my head."

"You have those walls all up around you. That's just as bad. Come a day you gonna want to tear them down brick by brick and gonna find that the cement is all hard. What you gonna do then?"

"I don't know what you're talking about. These walls are about as real as those talking dolls you said you had. You might think you know a lot, but it's all in your imagination."

"I never said I knew a lot. You said it. So it must mean I do. I know you want to ask me all kinds of questions about this baby, but you're too polite. Rich people don't do that, do they? They wait until someone offers up the information."

"I don't care anything about your being pregnant."

"Now, that's a lie. I saw how you was looking at my stomach when I got out of that car. And all during dinner you couldn't take your eyes off of me."

I didn't say anything. It was hard to believe how right she was.

64

"Well, go ahead, ask me. We got to live together for the next three months, so you might as well get all that stuff out of your system."

"I told you I don't care," I said as a thousand questions filled my mind. I wanted to know what had happened, how she'd gotten pregnant. I wanted to know where she and Danny had done it and how many times.

"You want to know if it's a boy or girl, right?" Then without waiting she said, "Well, it's a boy."

"How do you know—"

"Well, I didn't find out what it's gonna be, 'cause I can't keep it, but—"

"Why don't you want to keep him?"

"See, I knew you wanted to know."

"You just wanted to tell me, so you might as well go on."

"I don't want to be like my moms. She had to leave school because of me. And then all her friends went on to do all this cool stuff like your moms and Marion. When I first found out I was pregnant, I was going to keep him. But I could always have more," she said, pulling at the crocheted balls on her bedspread. "Anyway, the Robertses, that's that couple that can't have no kids, they're rich like you all, so he'll be happy."

"Just because you're rich doesn't mean you're happy," I said.

"Then trade beds with me."

"What?"

"Trade beds with me. You got that big bed with that soft

mattress. I know, 'cause I felt it. That's how your whole life's been, isn't it? All rich and soft."

"You must be crazy!"

"See, I knew you was selfish. Here I am all pregnant and you won't even give over your bed for one lousy night."

"Take it!" I said, pulling my pillows off the bed and walking over to Rebecca's side of the room. "Is that how you get your way—by manipulating?"

Rebecca picked up her pillow and headed for my bed, smirking. "Manipu-what?"

"Look it up!" I said, climbing in bed and turning away from her.

"Whatever it is," she whispered, "it works!"

In the darkness I gave Rebecca the finger and closed my eyes.

Twelve

"You know what dites do together?" Rebecca whispered loudly. She was closest to the window now, and I had to look past the outline of her stomach to see into the night, the attic smell of the mattress wafting up around me.

Downstairs, I heard Ma's key in the door, then the sound of her heels clicking toward the den.

"I don't *care*," I said.

"You know what *anybody* does together?"

"I don't care."

"You ever been with a boy?"

"You're so damned nosy. Why don't you go to sleep already? Isn't your baby tired?"

"No, he's not tired, and I'm telling your mother you cursed if you don't answer my questions."

"I don't care if you tell my mother," I lied.

"You too embarrassed to talk about it," Rebecca said.

"I don't want to talk about it with *you*. If anybody, I'd talk to Caesar."

"Who's Caesar? Your boyfriend?"

"Caesar's a girl. She's my best friend."

"Who'd name their girl Caesar?"

"Her parents."

"That's a boy's name. Where do rich people get these names from . . . Feni, Caesar . . ."

"She was named after somebody way down the line somewhere. Her dad said it's a strong name so she'd grow up to be strong."

"I want to meet her," Rebecca said.

"No."

"Why not? You embarrassed to have a pregnant girl in your house?"

"No. Caesar just doesn't come here, that's all."

"I'll bet you she comes here when she finds out about me."

"Bet you she won't."

"Hah!" Rebecca said smugly.

I turned away from Rebecca and changed the subject back. "I know what Marion and Bernadette do together. They love each other."

"Bernadette's that lady who's taking me to the doctor, right?"

"Yeah. She's going to be tutoring you too."

"Is Seton like Greenwich Village or something?"

"What's Greenwich Village?"

"This place in New York where a whole lot of gay people are."

"There're gay people everywhere."

"Well, I've met more here in one day than I met in New York in my whole life!"

"And you say *I'm* sheltered."

Rebecca was quiet for a moment. "So you think they really love each other?"

"They love each other more than my mother and dad. Marion and Bernadette are still together."

"You ever been with a boy?" she asked again.

"No."

"Why not?"

"I don't want to be!"

"You ever been with a girl?"

"No."

"Why not?"

"Same reason. I'm twelve! It's not a race!"

"Nobody said it was a race. I was just wondering. You saying I'm fast?"

"You said it. I didn't."

"You saying I shouldn't have done it?"

"I don't even know you. I don't care what you do."

"I think I shouldn't have gotten pregnant. I'm scared, you know. Scared to have this baby."

Outside, the wind whistled past the window and rattled the pane. Rebecca moved and her bedsprings squealed.

When my grandmother was a teenager, her best friend got pregnant. She kept the pregnancy hidden from everyone until it was time for the baby to come. Grandma was with her on the night the baby was born. But Grandma said that because her friend was so young, there were a lot of problems. And the baby died. I shivered and pulled the covers up over me. I knew what Rebecca was afraid of.

Thirteen

"I WANT TO MAKE A COLLECT CALL. MY NAME'S Rebecca."

I woke up the next morning to Rebecca's voice coming from the hallway and sat up in my bed. She hadn't even asked if she could use our phone!

"Danny! It's Rebecca! Accept the charges. . . . Danny!"

I heard the receiver slam and immediately heard Rebecca pick up the phone again and dial. "A collect call . . . Rebecca.

"Accept the charges. . . . Danny!"

The phone slammed down again and again I heard Rebecca dialing.

"Danny!" she cried. "What's wrong with you, man!"

There was a pause. "I don't care what your mama said about the phone bill. Tell your stupid sister to stop making all those nine-hundred calls! Now I'm gonna be owing these people money on their phone bill here and I ain't got it." She sucked her teeth. "Yeah. Yeah. Like you gonna send me everything else. Like we gonna run away and have this baby. Now I'm sitting up in these people's house and . . .

70

Danny! You should see this house. They got those new kind of faucets with only the one thing and you turn it left for hot and right for cold and they got *two* bathrooms! You know what else? They got that leather couch like you said we was going to get when you got everything together. They're rich, I'm telling you!" She listened for a while.

"She's okay. I think she's like eleven or twelve, but she acts like a baby. I don't even think she knows where babies come from. Her mother's nice, but the girl doesn't seem like she has any friends. I feel sorry for her."

"Me?" I said out loud, bolting straight up in bed. *She* was the pitiful one!

"Her old man cut out on them, then went somewhere else and started all over again. You know how that goes."

Telling our business to some stranger! I bounded out of bed and headed for the door.

"She's a pretty girl, though, in that innocent way. But I think she got one of those evil streaks in her, so I don't mess with her too much."

I stopped with my hand on the knob.

"The moms is pretty too. How's my old lady? She doing okay? You been by there to see her?" Rebecca paused again.

"I really 'preciate that. I miss you, Danny. You look after my sisters and brothers too. Let me give you the number here. These people seem cool, but call me in the day when the moms is at work."

She gave him the number, hung up, then dialed again.

"Collect to Clair from Rebecca . . . Thank you."

She whistled off-key while she waited. She couldn't whistle to save her life.

"Hi, Ma. How you feeling? No, I'm real good. Uh-huh, they're okay. Yes, Ma, I said thank you. I promise. You taking your nerve medicine? Is Dee's nose still running? That's good. Ma . . . tell everybody I miss them so much, okay? Tell them I'm going to come home soon. You take care of yourself too. I miss you the most." Rebecca sniffed and hung up the phone.

I leaned against the door and sighed, not knowing what I was feeling anymore. I had never hated someone and felt so sorry for them at the same time.

When I heard the bathroom door close, I opened my door and headed downstairs. Ma had left for work two hours earlier. There was a note for me and one for Rebecca. My note said, *Feni—Get to school on time. Here is some lunch money. Have a good day.* Beside the note there was a five-dollar bill. I stuck the money in my bathrobe pocket and crumpled up the note. Rebecca's note explained how to use the microwave and the contents of the refrigerator. There was no money beside it.

Rebecca came downstairs as I poured a bowl of Rice Krispies, her eyes red rimmed from crying. Her stomach stuck out from underneath her T-shirt, and light brown stretch marks showed on either side of her navel.

"You're staring again," she said dryly. I ducked my head and she set the teakettle on the stove and lit the burner beneath it.

"How far away is your school?"

"About five blocks. Why?"

"What grade does it go up to?"

"Why?"

"God, can't I just ask a question without you 'whying' me to death?"

I began munching my cereal silently.

"Just 'cause I want to know, Feni. Is that better?"

"Goes to twelfth."

Rebecca nodded and searched the cabinet.

"Tea is in that canister on the counter. We don't drink coffee." We didn't say anything. After a while, the kettle whistled.

"Anyways," she said, taking a cup from the mug rack and pouring hot water into it, "I was in the ninth grade before that stupid school gave me the dropkick. When I started showing, that pointy-headed principal called me into his office." She turned back toward me, leaned against the counter, and folded her arms above her stomach. " 'Well, now, Miss Rebecca,' " she said, deepening her voice, " 'seems to me you've gotten yourself into a little trouble.' By the time he finished talking all that junk, I would have left anyways, even if they hadn't kicked me out."

"You're going back to school after this, aren't you?"

"Of course."

"Then it's good that Bernadette's going to tutor you."

"Then it's good that Bernadette's going to tutor you," Rebecca mimicked. "You're a pain."

"Takes one to know one."

"But you have beautiful eyes. Anyone ever told you that?"

I blushed. "No."

"Well, you do. You got what they call 'bedroom eyes.' You know what that means?"

I shook my head.

She laughed that superior laugh of hers and finished fixing her tea. When she turned back toward me, I narrowed my "beautiful" eyes into slits.

"Uh-oh. I knew you was evil. Look how you looking at me. You could probably kill somebody. How come you so evil?"

"I'm not evil."

"What goes on inside your head when you walking around this house quiet as a snake, not saying nothing to nobody?"

"Nothing."

"You thinking evil thoughts, that's what you doing."

I rolled my eyes at her and put my bowl to my lips the way Ma hated. What right did she have coming into this house and trying to tell me what I thought?

"Your ma said after your grandmama died, you got all closed off and wouldn't talk to nobody."

"My mother didn't tell you that!"

"Sure did. In the car on the way here from the airport she said she took you to one of them specialist doctors and they said wasn't nothing wrong with your mouth. Then when people stopped worrying about it, you started up talking again. Now, why you just stop talking like that and drive your ma crazy?"

"Your mother's crazy, mine isn't."

A shadow crossed Rebecca's face. She swished her tea

74

around in her cup without saying anything. After a moment she went on as though I hadn't spoken. "If I had all this you got, I'd be talking a mile a minute."

"What all do I have?" I yelled, slamming my bowl against the table. Rebecca jumped, then calmly brought her cup to her lips and looked at me above it. "You come into my house and take half my room, then you and my mother and Marion get all chummy-chummy. . . ." I sat back, wanting to be anywhere but where I was.

"So that's what your problem is. You jealous. Well, I don't want your moms. She's cold. She doesn't care about people. She thinks life is a bunch of little notes and meetings. She thinks dinner is a waste of time. If I'm gonna have any mother, it's gonna be my crazy moms in Manhattan, because she loves me. And I ain't giving this baby up to no family that I think ain't gonna love it! I know they will. I would never have no kid that I couldn't love, and that's what your mother did, ain't it? Went and had a kid she didn't even want and can't give a hundred percent to. If I was you, I'd get on the phone with my daddy right now and say, 'Come get me, 'cause there ain't no love here for me'!"

"If she was all that, you think she would have taken your pregnant self in? Nope! My mother's strong! She's quiet and strong. And you—you're so stupid, you don't even know what love is!"

I left the kitchen while she was thinking up a smart remark and made my way up to my room. The last thing I wanted was for Rebecca to see me crying. Behind me, I heard her take a loud sip of tea and set her cup down heavily.

75

Fourteen

"I WANT TO GO LIVE WITH DAD," I SAID TO MA IN THE den that night. I had waited until dinner was over and Rebecca was stretched out in the living room in front of the pregnancy exercise video Marion had brought over.

Ma's pencil froze in midair. "What are you talking about? You barely speak to your father, and God knows what it takes to get you to go out West for a visit."

"Well, I want to speak to him now and I want to go live with him . . . in Colorado," I stuttered, nervous all of a sudden.

Ma stared at me. Then her face fell and she held her head in her hands. "Why, Feni? What's wrong with the way things are here?"

"Nothing. I just—I just think I'll be happier in Colorado. That's all." I had not seen her cry in a long time, and now my arms hung uselessly at my sides.

"Are you and Rebecca not getting along?"

"She's okay."

"If you're upset about the bedroom situation, I guess I can move her into the guest room. It's just so cold in there."

"Ma, it's not Rebecca or the room or anything. I just want to live with Dad!" My palms were beginning to sweat.

"I thought we were finally becoming friends, Feni."

When did that happen? And anyway, mothers aren't supposed to be your friends.

"Can I call him?"

She sighed, then pulled out her address book. Seeing how dejected she looked made my stomach queasy. I held my breath for a moment, then exhaled.

"I've been trying to do everything I could to make it comfortable for you here," she said, turning the pages slowly. "I've worked my fingers to the bone so that you could have everything you wanted. . . ."

"I do have everything . . . almost."

Ma stopped turning. Without looking at me she asked, "What's missing, Feni?"

I shrugged, and when she didn't turn around, I said, "You don't want me anyway. You want a career and stuff. You don't have time for a daughter."

Ma's chair swiveled around and she reached over and pulled me to her. "You listen to me, Afeni Harris. And you listen to me good!" Her breath was hot and angry against my face, but I didn't dare to pull away. "You know I grew up in a family of seven children! Seven children and one mother. No father. No anything! And before I was twelve years old, three of the seven children were dead. Before I was thirteen, my mother had died. I did everything I could to hold what was left of that family together. And we never hugged and kissed and goo-gooed 'I love you' to each other. But every one of us knew in our hearts how the other felt! And when the state came in and separated me from my three brothers, I knew that was the last I'd see of them, but we all knew we'd love each other for a long time. Don't you ever let me hear you say I don't love you, because if I'm not showing it with words, I'm showing it with actions! I didn't grow up saying it, so I can't start now. But 'I love you' is in every meal you eat, every piece of clothing you wear, and every clean sheet you sleep on!" She opened the address book and tore out the page with my father's address and number on it. "Here!" she said, thrusting the page into my sweaty palm. "Call him and maybe he'll say 'I love you' with words. But if he does, ask him to show it too!" She let go of my other hand and I walked toward the door.

"But . . . everything is about *you*," I said. "Work and AA meetings and bringing Rebecca here. It's all about what you have to do for yourself."

"No, Feni, you're wrong. It's also about what I do for *you*. I stopped drinking for both of us, but especially for you. I work so you don't ever have to do some fast-food something after school, so you can have dance lessons if you want them, skating and skiing and vacations and food. So you can have nice clothes and private schools and Jack and Jill—"

"I hate Jack and Jill."

"You just don't understand Jack and Jill."

"It's just about a bunch of kids being snobby."

"Feni, Jack and Jill is about black people taking care of

ourselves. When those Girl Scouts and Boy Scouts and Four-H clubs weren't letting our kids join, we made our own clubs just like we've always been doing."

"I guess—"

"Jack and Jill is about taking care of our own, and that's what bringing Rebecca here is about, what the Seton chapter of Alcoholics Anonymous with its all-black membership is about, what black sororities and fraternities are about, and the sooner you learn all of this, the better."

"I still don't like Jack and Jill," I mumbled.

"You don't have to. Just like you don't have to like dancing and skiing. That's why I don't always make you go. I just want you to experience it all, to get a taste of every little bit of the things I didn't get a chance to sample when I was a girl. If you think what I'm giving you is not enough, then fine, go live with Bernard."

"I don't want to anymore. I'm sorry," I said.

"Don't be," Ma said wearily. "I just want you to know that I *do* love you, Feni, and I *do* want you here with me. I'm just not the kind of mother who goes around saying it every day."

I backed out of the den and stood outside the door. The words began sinking in and settling my stomach. They made sense to me now. We were not some TV family where everything was perfect all the time. Dad wasn't here anymore, and it really didn't matter because when he was here, he was a stranger anyway. It was only me and Ma, and maybe we weren't so close. The thought made me sad. Other girls were close to their mothers. They did things together. But I liked being by myself and thinking thoughts no one else knew about, not even Ma. I was a true-blue loner, and maybe Ma was too. So we fit together like a jigsaw and came apart just as easily.

I stood outside the door for a long time. Then I looked at the paper in my hand once more before tearing it into a thousand pieces. I walked past Rebecca unnoticed as she grunted through a toe-touching exercise, and stuck my tongue out at her back.

Fifteen

"You have to come meet her, Caesar. I need some-one to hate her with."

At lunch Caesar and I sat in the crowded pizzeria on the corner sharing a calzone and Coke. Caesar's eyes were bright with excitement.

"I can't believe she's only fifteen," she said. "How old does she look?"

"I don't know. She thinks she's a grown-up just because she's pregnant."

"Can you imagine?" Caesar wondered aloud. "My mom would nail me to a cross!"

I took a big bite of calzone. "You know something? I don't think my mother would be all that mad. I just think she'd be really, really disappointed."

"*Your* mother?"

"Caesar, you know her from before. She's different now."

Caesar looked doubtful.

"Since she stopped drinking, she's a lot calmer. She still works a lot, though. But I think if I ever got pregnant, she'd take care of me. And Marion and Bernadette too.

Bernadette's over there tutoring Rebecca right now, and Marion bought all these nice clothes for her. She didn't have hardly anything when she came to stay with us."

"What happened to all her stuff?"

"Ma says they never really had anything."

"No clothes?"

"Her family doesn't have any money. It's a whole bunch of them living in four rooms."

"God! She probably never had her own room before now."

"That's the worst part. She's staying in *my* room. She's the last person I see before I go to sleep and the first person I see when I wake up!"

"Horror show!"

"The guest room is cold, and I threw a fit when Ma suggested Grandma's room."

"Yeah, that's too sacred, I guess."

"She's such a pain, Caesar. All she talks about is the baby and Danny."

"Who's Danny?"

"Her boyfriend."

"The baby's daddy?"

"Yeah."

"How old is he?"

"Seventeen."

"Seventeen! Can you imagine, Feni! I think I'd die."

"I don't think I'm ever going to get pregnant."

"I can't even think about *kissing* a boy, let alone going all the way and doing the wild thing!"

"Me either. They probably didn't even know how to do it right."

"Well, they knew how to do something right, 'cause she sure is pregnant."

We giggled.

"Afeni, can you imagine? Lying down naked beside somebody?"

"Kill myself."

"Double kill myself. Not in a trillion years. I don't even think I'll do it with my husband."

"You have to, Caesar. That's why they marry you."

"Well, he's just going to have to marry me for my brains, because no way, José, am I going to ever take off my clothes in front of somebody. I don't even let my mom see me naked!"

"I saw Rebecca with no shirt on," I whispered, and Caesar's eyes opened wide.

"What'd she look like? Did she look like—like us?"

"Uh-uh. Everything's so swollen. Her stomach sticks way out and her breasts are gigantic."

"That's because of the milk. They're getting ready for it to come."

"I know *that*."

"Was anything else different?"

I nodded. "From the neck down she looks like she's thirty. But then you look at her face and you know she's only a kid like us."

Caesar looked at the calzone, then pushed it back toward me.

"When she caught me looking," I continued, "she started screaming, 'Stop staring at me! You're always staring!' "

"Well, of course you have to stare!" Caesar agreed.

"I just know the sooner she's gone the better."

"I wish I could meet her. I never saw a pregnant teenager."

"You should come over."

"I don't know, Feni. . . ."

"Why don't you come after school sometime? My mother won't be around. Anyway, she's really sorry about what happened, Caesar. She really has changed."

"Maybe. I think I'll roll over and die if I don't meet her."

"How about Monday?"

"Jack and Jill is having a dinner dance."

"On a Monday afternoon? That club is so stupid. I'm so glad Ma doesn't make me go!"

"Yeah . . . how come you don't have to go anymore?"

"Ma says if I come straight home, now that Rebecca's there, it'll be okay. What a choice—Rebecca or Jack and Jill."

"It's fun, Feni."

"I hate all that stuff."

"You'll like it when you do cotillion. Then we'll be sixteen. It'll be different."

"I'm not doing cotillion, because I'm not coming out. I think that's all bull. All you do is wear a stupid gown and get all your friends to look just as dumb."

"I like wearing stupid gowns."

"Sorry."

"That's okay."

"Then come Tuesday."

"Maybe. We better get back." Caesar took a last bite of calzone and stood to put her coat on. "You talk to your father lately?"

"No," I said, not mentioning the fight Ma and I had had the week before.

"You're still mad, aren't you?"

"He's such a jerk! How could you forget how old your own daughter is?"

"That is pretty jerky. You ever going to go to Colorado for a visit again?"

"No."

"They have some good skiing there."

"There's good skiing here. Anyway, I hate skiing."

We headed back toward Roper silently, walking slowly because the sun felt so good on our faces.

"Does Rebecca go to private or Catholic school?" Caesar asked at the door.

"She went to a public school. But they kicked her out when she got pregnant."

"Public school. My father says the public schools in New York are real bad. There was an article in the *Times* once about how many kids were shot and stabbed in those schools."

"They don't have money for private school."

"I wonder what happened to their money."

"They never had any, Caesar. Read my lips. Her family doesn't have *any* money!"

"Wow. Who's going to pay for her cotillion?"

"She can have mine!"

85

Sixteen

"WHO'S JANIE FEEDLER?" REBECCA ASKED OUT OF THE blue a week later.

"What?"

"Janie Feedler. Who is she?"

I was sitting on my bed reading. It was Saturday, and Rebecca had spent the morning trying to persuade me to show her around Seton. Me, Ma, Marion, and Bernadette had already shown her the library, the railroad station, and Seton's one museum, but today I had no plans to leave the house. Not only was it below zero outside, but more snow had fallen during the night. The warmest place in the house, next to the fireplace, was my room.

"She's a neighbor. Why?"

"I heard your mother on the telephone with Marion. She said Janie Feedler had asked if I was at your house for charity reasons."

I rolled my eyes. "She's a crotchety something. Never minds her business. What did Ma say?"

"She said that she told her I was a good friend of yours and then the nosy crotchety—what's crotchety?"

86

"It's like crabby, rickety, something like that."

"Well, anyway, Ms. Feedler asked her if I was in trouble and your mother said, 'No, Rebecca's not in any trouble at all.' "

"Ma said that?"

Rebecca nodded. "That's wild, isn't it?"

"You shouldn't be listening," I said.

"I *overheard*. Don't be so crotchety, Feni! What kind of name is Feni anyway?"

"It's Swahili," I said, turning back to my book, amazed at how fast Rebecca could jump from one thing to the next.

"Swahili for what? You don't just go giving somebody a name because it's some sort of African thing. It should have a meaning." She lay back on her bed and stared up at the ceiling. Every now and then she went over to the window and looked, then fell back on her bed again. I wondered what she was expecting to see different out there.

After a while I said, "It's short for Afeni, which means 'the Dear One.' "

" 'The Dear One'!" Rebecca laughed. " 'The Dear One'!"

"What's so funny about that?" I asked, slamming the book closed.

"The Dear One! That's what's so funny! You ain't dear at all!"

"Maybe not to you. But somebody thought I was! I don't care what you think!"

"Who thought you was dear?" she asked, calming down and raising herself up on her elbow.

87

"My grandmother named me," I said, fingering the pages of my book.

"Is that your grandmother that died?" Rebecca asked, her eyes all questions and interest.

I nodded. "She got killed in California when I was eight."

"How?"

I recounted the bus-incident story for Rebecca and watched as her face masked over in horror.

"I miss her," I whispered, feeling tears well up in the back of my throat.

Rebecca lay back on her bed and took a deep breath. She rested her hands on her high stomach. "Is she the girl in the frame you put on the night table every single night?"

I felt for the small silver frame in my back pocket and nodded—then, realizing Rebecca had been snooping through my things, started to say something. But Rebecca spoke before I could.

"That's deep. That must be why it's like you have this gigantic wall built up around you with a sign on the front saying go away."

"I don't know what you're talking about," I said, picking up my book again. Here I had just told her about my grandmother, when I had never talked about it to anyone before, and now she was talking about some walls somewhere!

"Come here!" she said excitedly.

I looked over at her holding her stomach. "Is the baby

coming?" I asked, putting down my book and heading toward the door, ready to call Ma if she started screaming.

"No!" She gasped. "I want you to feel this."

"Feel what?" I took small steps toward her bed. She reached out for my hand and pressed it against her stomach. Something jutted out and I tried to snatch my hand away, but Rebecca held it firmly.

"Something's moving!"

"It's the baby! He's kicking! He wants to get out of there soon." Rebecca laughed. "Don't be scared of it. He ain't gonna bite you!"

I relaxed a little and felt the soft skin on her stomach move back and forth beneath my hand.

"That's for your grandmother," Rebecca said. "People die to make space for other people to live. Now that your grandma is gone, somebody else got to come in the world."

I frowned, not believing her.

"It's true," she said. "Babies come down from heaven—only, they take the long way—and while they're on their way down, the other people that been here already are heading on up there."

"That's bull," I said, getting up and going back over to my bed. Somewhere in the back of my mind, though, I wanted to believe every word of it.

"So you don't have to be building up walls and shutting people out, 'cause everything works out okay."

"You sure think you know a lot for a fifteen-year-old. If you know so much, how come you got yourself in trouble?"

"I told you before, this ain't trouble. Ask that family that's taking my baby if it's trouble. And I know a lot because I seen a lot. You can't be growing up in New York City and not know a lot. Every day, something new happening around there. They got a lot of drugs and killing where I live. . . ."

"You took drugs before?"

Rebecca shook her head. "I don't need that junk. My boyfriend, though, he was smoking a lot, but when me and him got together, he stopped. But I got too much stuff going on to be losing my head with nobody's drugs. And plus I got love. My boyfriend loves me, and my ma and my sisters and brothers love me. That's about all I need, you know?"

"You and your boyfriend gonna get married?"

Rebecca laughed that grown-up laugh of hers. "You're full of questions today, aren't you? When I came here, you was all eyes and silence. I like you better when you're talking. Nah, though. Me and my boyfriend got bigger plans than marriage."

"What kind of plans?"

"Oh, all kinds," she said. "Houses and cars and picket-fence plans."

"Well, how come he never calls you? I heard you talking to him on the phone that morning. And you gave him our number and everything."

She hesitated a moment. "He calls while you at school."

I knew she was lying but didn't say anything.

"And anyway, you shouldn't be listening to other people's conversations. Even if this is your house."

I picked up my book and opened it to the folded-down page, staring at the words without reading them.

"My boyfriend is going to buy me all kinds of things," Rebecca was saying. "When I get home, we all gonna party and celebrate."

"Just like your friends are going to write you all the time."

There was a long silence, and when I looked up, Rebecca was staring out the window again, her back straight, her shoulders shaking. "Why don't you just leave other people's business alone? Why you gotta be so mean, anyway?"

Seventeen

WE DIDN'T SPEAK FOR A WEEK. MA AND MARION LEFT
us alone, prodded Rebecca with questions about the baby
and me with questions about school. Our answers were
monosyllabic between questions, our meals were silent.
One night I turned from the television to catch Ma staring
at the two of us, sitting far away from each other. She
called me into the den.

"How was school today?" she asked.

"Fine," I said, playing with the frames she had above her
computer. All the pictures were of me at different stages—
crawling, walking, eating, kindergarten graduation.

"What's going on out there?" Ma asked, gently pulling
my hands into her own.

"Nothing," I said, too casually. "You know how people
get when they're pregnant."

"Oh?" Ma cocked an eyebrow, a smile playing at the
corners of her mouth. "How's that?"

"Crabby about things," I said.

"You two going to work it out?"

I shrugged. "Guess so. She doesn't get in my way and I
won't get in hers."

"Well, I guess I'll let you handle this yourselves. No need for me to come between friends, is there?"

"We're not friends!" I said.

Ma let go of my hands and pulled one of my braids.

"I'll let you two handle it," she said again.

I stormed into the living room and sat on the couch—as far away from Rebecca as I could get.

"I don't want to watch any stupid pregnancy exercise junk," I said.

Saying nothing, Rebecca picked up both remotes, clicked off the VCR, and flipped through the channels. She stopped at a show on public television about dolphins. The man speaking was saying that there was a chance dolphins might be as smart as humans. He stared into the screen as he said this, and his blue eyes bored holes into us. Then a woman came on, promising they'd continue the show after they had collected another thousand dollars and pleading with us to call in and pledge money. I sneaked a look at Rebecca, and although her eyes were glued to the screen, they did not stop there, but moved on past it into a place I couldn't see.

"I think maybe the baby is dying," she said.

The words echoed off the TV woman's soft pleading and settled in my stomach. I was not sure whether or not Rebecca was talking to me, but felt I should answer anyway.

"Why do you think that?"

When Rebecca finally answered, her voice was soft, clear, and full of sadness.

"He used to move around so much, and now he doesn't hardly move at all."

"Maybe it's because you're exercising and doing school-work with Bernadette and everything. Maybe he's just tired."

Rebecca shook her head. "It's not that," she said. "He knows."

"Knows what?" I asked quietly. In a minute the man and the dolphins would be back on. I didn't want Rebecca to stop talking. I had missed her.

"He knows we're not in Harlem no more and that he's going to go live with somebody that's not really his mother."

"Don't worry, Rebecca. It's going to be okay." I was unsure. I had not thought much about what would happen when the baby came and Rebecca went home again. Nor had I thought about the baby actually being born. That had all seemed like such a long time away. But now, Rebecca had been here more than a month, and the baby would be here in another six weeks. Then Rebecca would stay a little while longer and that would be the end. "Don't worry, Rebecca," I said again, because I didn't know what else to say.

"The doctor says he's healthy, but I know that's not true. I try to eat good, and I talk to him at night. I whisper so I don't wake you up. And he used to kick a little to let me know he heard every word. But he doesn't do that no more. He hardly kicks at all now. And yesterday I was bleeding a little. You know what that means?"

I shook my head, but Rebecca was staring at the screen and didn't see me. "No."

"You not supposed to bleed when you're pregnant. It means something is real wrong inside."

"Maybe he's just sleeping more."

The man and the smart dolphins came back on the screen, and Rebecca watched the dolphins jump through hoops and sing dolphin songs. The man said dolphins laugh like humans and understand stuff. He said dolphins cry.

Rebecca rubbed her stomach. Her face had gotten chubbier, and the short curls had grown down over her eyes. She chewed a hangnail as she watched.

"Monday, Marion's taking me to Dr. Greenberg again so she can listen to the baby's heart. She says if I want, she'll tell me whether it's a boy or girl. I told her don't tell me."

"You think there's a teeny-tiny chance it might be a girl?"

"Nope," Rebecca said stubbornly. "Danny's calling me tomorrow."

I wondered why she was telling me all of this.

"He's going to call around three-thirty. You want to show me around Seton some more after I get off the phone, or are you afraid to be seen with me without your ma and Marion?"

"I don't care about being seen with you. I don't care what people think."

"Then you'll show me? I've seen a lot of buildings and I wondered what they were."

"I'll show you."

"Now we're friends again, right?" Rebecca turned to me

for the first time that evening. She smiled and her dimples cut deeply into her cheeks, making her look a lot younger than fifteen.

"Yeah, we're friends, I guess."

"You really think dolphins are as smart as humans?" I asked when the man promised to show us a dolphin giving birth.

Rebecca stared at the screen. The fund-raising woman came back on, asking for another thousand, and Rebecca got up and switched the television off. She pulled the elastic waistband down below her belly before she sat down again. "I think that stupid man is lying," she said. "He knows dolphins are way smarter than any human!"

Eighteen

WHEN DANNY CALLED SATURDAY, I DID MY BEST NOT to eavesdrop but still couldn't help overhearing snatches of the conversation.

"Ma and I talk almost every day, so you don't have to give me the lowdown on the whole neighborhood," Rebecca said into the phone from the upstairs hallway. From the living room, where I sat waiting for her, I could hear her clearly if I listened real hard.

"She told me Nikki was pregnant now but she's not gonna have it." There was a long pause. "She too young to be having babies anyway," Rebecca said softly.

Five minutes later, after what seemed like a hundred I-love-you's and other corny stuff, she hung up and we were on our way.

For six blocks the back of my throat burned with the question I had been dying to ask her for a long time. Rebecca chatted on and on about Danny and her friends in Harlem. She compared the brownstones in West Harlem with the small houses along the side streets in Seton. She laughed at the names of things—Hallerton Five and Dime, Beagle Road, Window Tree Lane—and told me stories about her brothers and sisters.

"Now, Bobo and Shaunney, they're identical twins," she said about the youngest in her family. "We used to make Shaunney wear a green ribbon around his wrist so we could tell them apart. Sometimes they'd switch and Bobo would wear the ribbon. Confuse everybody in the house except Ma."

"Who would name their kid Bobo?"

"His real name is Elwood, but we gave him that nickname. All the kids get nicknames in Harlem—Bobo, Booboo, CeeCee, Little Man."

"Who names them?"

"Anybody. People down the street, upstairs from you. Next-door neighbors. They say, 'Now, who he look like? Don't he favor Leon's grandson, Bud? Come here, Li'l Bud.' And the next thing you know, that's your nickname."

"What was your nickname?"

Rebecca looked embarrassed.

"Come on," I said. "I won't tell anybody."

"Swear?"

"Cross my heart, hope to die." I drew a cross on my chest with my index finger and pointed it toward heaven.

"Stinky," she whispered.

"Stinky! Why'd they name you something like that?"

Rebecca shrugged, but I knew she knew the answer.

We laughed for nearly a block, until the tears streaming down our faces came close to freezing.

At the corner of Agauma and Seventh Street I took a

deep breath, shoved my hands in my pockets, and looked at her.

"How come you decided to have the baby?" I asked.

Rebecca looked at me like she had been waiting a month and a half for this question. "I didn't tell anybody I was pregnant," she said, pulling her scarf closer to her throat. "I knew it, but I was real, real scared. I wasn't sure what I was going to do. So I just kept it hidden. It was easy because I always wear baggy clothes anyway."

"How'd Clair finally find out?"

"She walked in on me in the bathroom. By then I was something like five and a half months. Man . . . my ma hit the roof in four different directions, she was so mad."

"Then what happened?"

Rebecca looked down at the cracks in the sidewalks. "Then we both started crying. Me sitting there in the bathtub, Ma sitting on the toilet. We just cried and cried and cried. Like everything we ever had was all gone."

"That must have been real scary."

She shook her head. "By then I wasn't scared no more. I was just sorry for what I had done and real sorry for hurting Ma."

"Didn't you and Danny . . ." I hesitated. "Didn't you have any . . . you know . . . like condoms or something?"

Rebecca shook her head again. "We were planning to get something. We were going to go to the free clinic down on St. Marks Place and stuff. But we had taken chances before and nothing happened. I guess we thought we could just take another chance. It was stupid."

99

"That's too bad," I said.

"Everything happens for a reason," Rebecca said, sounding old and convinced.

We walked a long way in silence, pictures of Rebecca and Clair crying in the bathroom popping in and out of my head.

Nineteen

THE NEIGHBORHOOD OF SHACKS IS THE SMALL STRETCH of land clear across the back roads of Seton where poor white people live. The shacks are small tin and tar houses with roofs slanting toward the street. The shacks' windows are holes cut into the tin and filled with plastic. Before the poor families settled into them years ago, they had been the homes of squatters and coal miners, people passing through Seton with no plans to stay. Where the shacks stop, behind the high hills that curve around to hide them, black doctors and lawyers and bankers and public-relations people settled. With their families they hid themselves away from the shacks. A lot of kids in my neighborhood have never seen the back roads, or, as they call them, the shack roads. School buses stay down in the valleys on the other side or take the roads up on the hills, so that if you're riding in one and look down, all you see is the slanted line of houses. Not the littered streets. Not the half-naked kids with dirty necks. Not the stray animals turning over garbage cans.

We stumbled on the neighborhood of shacks by accident. We had been touring Seton all day. I'd shown Rebecca the stores, Roper Academy, the gardens. But it was Saturday and Roper Academy was cold red boring stone. Closed. The gardens were flat with ice and snow, stretching for a mile and a half. Rebecca had grown restless quickly, and it was then that we saw him—a pale little boy in a ragged coat who couldn't have been more than four years old.

"He must've gotten lost," Rebecca said, moving toward him.

"He probably didn't," I said. "Kids around here walk around like that. They look for junk in the garbage cans."

"How's some mother gonna let a kid that small out in this cold weather to look in garbage cans? Answer me that!"

I shrugged, walking briskly to keep up with her. "That's the way the people are around here."

"You sound like a snob! A kid's a kid."

"I don't like it over here, Rebecca. I'm going back."

"You scared of this side of town? Is this what you were afraid to show me?"

"Of course not. It's just dirty. It smells funny over here."

A girl came out from one of the shacks and started walking toward us. Her dirty blond hair hung limply above her shoulders, and the side of her pale face was streaked as though, busy with a more important task, she had dragged a dirty hand across it to scratch an itch.

"Jason! Jason-Eliot. You get over here now, boy!"

"Mama!" the boy screamed, running over to the girl.

Rebecca froze. The girl couldn't have been more than fifteen.

She held on to the boy and stared at me through half-closed eyes. I was wearing the leather bomber jacket I had gotten last Christmas. She looked at the sleeves, at the suede collar, at the wool pants I wore beneath it. Her stare stopped at my boots, made its way up to my jacket again, and stopped again somewhere just below my nose, more hate in her eyes than I have ever seen. The ragged child beside her put his thumb in his mouth and wrapped his other arm around her legs.

"You don't live around here," she said to me. "There's no coloreds livin' over 'cross this side."

"Coloreds!" Rebecca laughed. "I haven't heard that since *Roots.*" She looked around, then looked back at the girl and down at the little boy. "Thank God we don't," she said, glaring at the girl. "We just brought your baby back."

"He know his way," the girl said, prying the baby's hand from her leg.

The girl looked at Rebecca. Her gaze traveled over Rebecca's ragged scarf and down to her protruding stomach. Something in her eyes caught and she nearly smiled. "Come on, Jason-Eliot. I told you 'bout roaming the trash."

"You're welcome," Rebecca called as the girl and Jason-Eliot turned and headed in the opposite direction.

We started walking back toward my neighborhood.

"It ain't so bad," the girl called. We turned back to see that she had stopped and was holding Jason-Eliot in her arms. "Once those pains come, it's almost over. After that

103

it ain't so bad." Then she turned again and continued down the gray snow and ice path toward the slanted shacks.

Rebecca and I turned back and silently headed up the high hills toward home.

Twenty

WHEN MA CAME HOME LATE MONDAY NIGHT WITH A pizza, Marion, Bernadette, Rebecca, and I were doing breathing exercises, sitting four across, Native American style, in front of the television.

"Come join us," Bernadette said, her forehead shiny with sweat beneath her braids.

Bernadette's mother and father moved here from Kenya soon after they married. Wanting to Americanize as quickly as possible, they moved to the Long Island suburbs, had two children, and named them Thomas and Bernadette. Even now, when Bernadette tells the story, she laughs about it. And even though I've heard the story at least a thousand times, I can sit through it another thousand just to catch the spark in Bernadette's dark eyes when she recounts it, just to play with the cornrows gliding down her back while she tells it.

"You were supposed to hold it for a count of ten, Bernadette."

"No way. When you get to be my age, the count goes down to six."

"Same here," Marion said, rising. "I can't even breathe as deeply as that lady on the screen. She must have a set of lungs on her!"

"You smoke too much," Rebecca scolded, closing her eyes and pressing her hands against her stomach.

"Thanks, Clair Junior," Marion said, following Bernadette into the kitchen.

"Marion and Bernadette make a nice couple," Rebecca whispered.

"They've been together long enough."

"If the Robertses hadn't asked for the baby first, I'd give him to them."

I blinked. "You've come a long way. When you first came here, you didn't even like Marion!"

"I didn't know her," Rebecca said. "How you gonna judge someone you don't know?"

I smirked. "Now you do the short exhales and I count, Rebecca," I said, pressing the mute button.

"Okay."

We did the exercise four times.

"I'm starved," Marion was saying to Ma in the dining room. "Pour Rebecca a larger glass of milk, Catherine. And put an iron pill beside her plate."

"I thought she only took these in the morning."

"Dr. Greenberg said she needs to take one at night too."

"What else did she say?"

Ma was putting another plate at the end of the table when we sat down.

"She said the baby's fine," Rebecca said, searching for a

comfortable position in the straight-back chair. "He's just moving slower these days. She said there's a chance the baby might be premature because I'm so young or something."

"Did she recommend anything?"

"Bed rest," she said, taking a slice of pizza from the box and picking off a chunk of cheese. "My blood pressure is too high. She said it's too much excitement for me." Her look said, *That's a joke.*

"You have to stay in bed for a month?" I asked.

Rebecca nodded. "At least, stay around the house."

"Well, what about your breathing classes?" Ma asked.

"She said I shouldn't worry about that right now. The baby will come whether I take classes or not."

"What about studying?" Bernadette asked.

"I guess I can't do that either. Especially math—"

"Studying's fine, Bernie," Marion interrupted. "Just so long as it doesn't mean long walks through Seton and heavy lifting."

"Ah-haaa. Got you!" I laughed.

Rebecca smirked.

"And what about the Robertses?" Ma asked. "Have you spoken to them?"

"Who're the Robertses?"

"They're the ones adopting the baby, Feni. Those people I told you about," Rebecca said. "They're coming by to see me a week from Wednesday. Hope that's cool with you."

"It's fine," Ma said, Bernadette and Marion nodding in

unison. "We just want you to be sure you're making the right decision. I know you don't want to raise a baby where you're living now, but there are some beautiful places there in Harlem. I'm not trying to talk you into keeping him or anything. I just don't want you to think you made the wrong choices."

"I know there are beautiful places, but not where I live. I have to take care of my brothers and sisters. I don't think I could raise a baby right. I wouldn't want him to have to live off welfare like we gotta do now. It would be too much. I know in my heart it isn't the right time now. Danny, he's cool and everything, but he's only seventeen. He's not ready to be nobody's daddy."

"You sound like you know what you want," Ma said. After a moment she added, "And I'm glad you're here."

"I'm glad too," Bernadette said.

"Count me in," Marion added, raising her hand.

Rebecca looked up at them, her face a mixture of embarrassment and pride.

Ma picked up her slice and rose. "I need to go make some phone calls so I can be home Wednesday morning. I'll drop Feni off at school and head back over here."

"You're not working on a Wednesday, Ma?"

"I'll work at home. I want to be here to meet the Robertses."

"Can't I stay home too? I haven't missed school all year. Please, Ma?"

"Can she, Ms. Harris?" Rebecca pleaded. "Please."

Ma sighed. "I guess so. How'd you do on that history test?"

"Ninety-eight."

Rebecca shot me a smarty-pants look.

"I figured you must have done well, since I didn't hear anything from Roper. You can stay home if Rebecca doesn't mind."

"No. It'll be cool. We're friends now."

Marion and Bernadette looked up, and Ma, heading toward her den, stopped halfway across the floor. "Friends?" she asked.

I picked some of the cheese off Rebecca's slice, looked her square in the eye, and nodded.

Twenty-one

A WEEK LATER CAESAR CAME HOME WITH ME AFTER school. All the way home she talked about the cotillion.

"I've decided to wear a blue gown," she said as we headed up Bailey Street. "Don't you think blue would look great on me? Blue with lace. I want lots of lace. What color do you think you'll wear?"

"Caesar, I told you. I'm not coming out."

"Your mother's going to make you do it."

"My mother doesn't care about that junk. That was my father, and he's gone now. He can make his new daughter come out if he wants, but not me."

"It's going to be so fun. Remember Vanessa, who's at Howard now?"

I shook my head. "Uh-uh."

"Well, hers was so beautiful. She wore yellow. She looked so pretty, Feni. The dress was cut in a V in the back, but I think I want a high collar. Maybe I'll wear white instead of blue."

At my door Caesar stopped talking and looked around nervously. "You sure your mother isn't home?"

"Positive," I said, taking out my keys. "She's working."

"Do I look okay?"

"You look fine, Caesar."

"Wait," she said, grabbing my hand. "Are you sure she'll like me? I mean, maybe I should come over some other—"

"Caesar. Don't worry. She's not a monster, just a pain sometimes."

"You think she'll tell us how it felt?"

"No. And don't ask!"

Rebecca was watching cartoons when we came in. Caesar glanced around, then walked over to the top of the two steps that lead down into the living room. "Is that her?" she whispered.

"Yes, it's me," Rebecca said. She turned, she and Caesar taking each other in from head to toe.

"Is it show-and-tell day?" Rebecca said finally, turning back to the television.

"Where's Bernadette?" I asked, pulling Caesar's coat off her shoulders while she stared.

"She had to leave early. She teaches on Tuesday nights."

"I'm Caesar," Caesar finally stuttered, moving slowly toward Rebecca.

"I know," Rebecca said, not turning away from the TV. "And I know you know who I am."

"Feni told me a-about you. She said you were, ahm, she said—"

"She told me the same things about you." Rebecca leaned back against the couch, smirking.

111

"You're supposed to be in bed, Rebecca." I hung Caesar's coat on the rack.

"I can't stay," Caesar said. "You don't look so young," she said to Rebecca. "I hope you have a girl."

"It doesn't matter what it is," Rebecca said. "I just want it to be healthy."

"Then I hope it's a healthy girl. Can I touch your stomach?"

"Caesar!"

"I was waiting for her to offer, but she didn't and I have to go."

"Sure, I guess." Rebecca looked at me, raising an eyebrow.

I shrugged.

Caesar took small steps closer to Rebecca. They looked at each other a moment before she reached out to touch Rebecca's stomach.

"That's the coolest thing I've ever felt," she said, smiling. "Is it going to hurt?"

"It hurts now!" Rebecca said. "Didn't you feel that kick? This baby isn't playing."

"I think I would absolutely die!" Caesar said, reaching out to touch Rebecca's stomach again.

"No, you won't die," Rebecca said softly.

A chill ran through me then. Caesar looked up, fear in her eyes.

"You'll just have your baby, start your family, and move on," Rebecca continued.

"Not me! Never!"

"Hah!" Rebecca laughed. "That's what everybody says."

"Even you?" I asked, coming to stand beside them.

"Yup! Even me!"

"My mother says when you get pregnant you throw up a lot. Gross!" Caesar stuck her finger in her mouth and faked a gag.

"I didn't get sick a whole lot. Just the first two or three weeks. Something like that."

"What'd your mother say?" Caesar nosed.

"She didn't know. I always turned the water on."

"What happened when she found out?"

"I thought you had to go, Caesar," I said.

"Why you have to leave so fast?" Rebecca asked.

"Jack and Jill is planning its regional conference and I'm on the committee. We have a meeting today."

"What's Jack and Jill?" Rebecca shifted on the floor and pressed the creases in the fabric on her stomach flat.

"A dumb club that all the kids go to."

"It's not dumb," Caesar said. "It's only for black kids, and we have dances and talent shows and go on trips and stuff."

"We go to places where we can *meet the right kinds of people,*" I mimicked.

"Feni!"

"Well, that's what it's about, Caesar."

"Sounds snobby," Rebecca said.

"It's not snobby. It's fun."

"It is fun, sometimes," I said, not wanting to betray Caesar. "Once we all saw *Porgy and Bess* and ate at a real French restaurant."

"And remember when we had that dance last year, and

all the girls danced together so then the chaperons got all mad."

We giggled and slapped our palms together. Rebecca smiled, uncertain.

"So it's like a club," she said, "for little rich kids?"

"We're not *rich*!" I nearly shouted.

"Yeah," Caesar agreed. "We just have stuff."

"Whatever," Rebecca said, waving her hand. "I don't think we have Jake and Jack in New York."

"Jack and Jill," Caesar corrected.

"Whatever."

"You want to come to my cotillion?" Caesar asked.

"What's that, a party?"

"Sort of. It's a coming out."

"That's like when you're introduced to everyone," I added.

"Who are they introducing you to?"

"Everyone!" Caesar said, throwing up her hands.

"All the other children of doctors and lawyers and bankers," I said.

"Oh."

"You want to come, Rebecca?"

"When is it?"

"In four years when I'm sixteen."

"Let me think about it," Rebecca said.

"Okay, but let me know soon," Caesar said, rising. "I'm making a list now."

"Are you sure I'm a 'right kind of person'?"

Caesar waved her hand. "Of course. Mine is going to be all cool kids and rap music."

"Yeah, right," I said. "They always make you play classical stuff."

"Only when you come down the stairs," Caesar said. "That's so people don't get distracted watching you make your entrance."

At the door Caesar turned. "I don't think you're a pain," she said.

Rebecca looked at me and raised an eyebrow. I wanted to die on the spot.

After Caesar left, I sat on the floor beside Rebecca. The television cast blue shadows over the living room. Rebecca pressed the mute button and turned to me.

"She's nice, but she seems a little bit . . . I don't know— like she doesn't know a whole lot about stuff. You know, like, sheltered. She's different from you—"

"Nah," I said. "I think Caesar and I are pretty much alike."

Rebecca shook her head. "Even though sometimes you don't act like it, Feni, you know things. You're down on what's up out there." Rebecca paused and pointed toward the window. "I don't think Caesar's ma would've let me stay at her house. Your moms is different. She's open to things, and she makes sure you're up on them too."

"Yeah, me and Ma talk about a lot of stuff."

"Caesar's different, though. Like I bet she wouldn't know Harlem if she tripped in front of the Apollo."

"Caesar's a good friend," I said.

"Yeah, she's cool. I like her. It's just I wish—I wish all the kids in Harlem could live in Seton for a month and all the kids in Seton could live in Harlem for a month. I think people would be different then, all around. Are all the kids at Roper like Caesar?"

"I don't know a lot of the kids. I guess everybody's parents want to protect them. Ma's different. She doesn't think I should not be exposed to things. She doesn't want me to grow up narrow-minded. Caesar's the only one I really talk to."

"Why?" Rebecca leaned back and rested her hands on her stomach.

"'Cause she's the only one who talks to me."

"You like having only one friend?"

"I have two now."

"But I'm not gonna always be around."

I shrugged, feeling my stomach tighten. "I don't need a lot of people."

"That's true," Rebecca said. "That's what I like about you. You take care of yourself. Some people need all these big groups and everything to make them feel like they're cool. Me and you aren't like that."

"But you say you have a lot of friends in Harlem."

"Yeah, I guess. I miss them too. But I don't really need them the way some people need their friends."

"My grandmother was my best friend. Look!" I took the picture frame out of my back pocket and handed it to Rebecca. "Remember when you snooped through my room and found this?"

She opened it and stared at the picture for a long time.

"Yeah, I remember. She sure was beautiful."

"She was the greatest. We were like this." I held up two

fingers and crossed them. "Nobody's ever going to get that close to me again."

"You can't always be pushing people away. Someday nobody'll come back."

I took the frame back from her and stared at Grandma, wiping off the prints on the glass with my shirt.

"Nobody will get close to me," I whispered, realizing that Rebecca already had.

Twenty-two

MR. AND MRS. ROBERTS ARRIVED AT EXACTLY TEN o'clock Wednesday morning. Rebecca was on the phone with Danny but hung up quickly and stumbled downstairs when the bell rang. At the door I was greeted by a bouquet of flowers, the man behind the flowers smiling. When he spoke, his voice made me feel warm and safe.

"My name is Ramón Roberts. This is my wife," he said, pushing a short, heavy woman in ahead of him. She smiled and took my hand.

"I'm Feni."

Her hands were small and warm, even though it was cold outside.

Rebecca's eyes opened wide at the sight of the flowers. She looked as though she would burst with pleasure.

Ma came out of the den and introduced herself.

"This is a beautiful neighborhood," Mr. Roberts said when everyone had settled in the living room. I was in the kitchen making tea but could hear every word. "So many trees and pretty houses."

"Where are you living?" Ma asked, sizing up the

Robertses. I liked them immediately, and that was a good sign.

"We're in Queens. It's residential. Lots of black folks. Good schools. But Barbara, she wants to move out to the country, in the mountains, someday."

"This is a nice place to have a family," Rebecca said.

"Is this where you would raise a family?" Mr. Roberts asked.

Rebecca must have nodded.

"Then I guess we'd better start looking at houses in the country," Mr. Roberts said.

I came back out with a tray of sugar, milk, and tea—peppermint tea for Rebecca and Mrs. Roberts, caffeinated for the rest of us.

Mrs. Roberts was sitting beside Rebecca with Rebecca's hand pressed between both of hers. "We wanted to come out here sooner. You've been here awhile."

"Two months," I said, but when everyone turned to look at me, I added quickly, "but it doesn't seem that long."

Rebecca smiled and Mrs. Roberts continued. "We both had to put in for vacation time. So now we're free for six weeks."

"Where are you staying?" Ma asked.

"Oh, we subletted someone's place over near the stores. It's a nice place. Big. No problem getting here from there."

"Do you like Seton?" Mr. Roberts asked Rebecca. "I mean, for yourself."

I held my breath.

"It's nice for families," she said. "I miss home."

It was then that I realized Rebecca would be leaving soon. I had not thought about it in a while, hoping Rebecca would like Seton enough to stay.

"We're going to look at real estate here," Mr. Roberts was saying. "Don't have any roots, really, in Queens. We'll be starting out fresh with the baby. Almost like newlyweds." He winked and Mrs. Roberts blushed.

"You think you might raise the baby here?" I asked, nearly spilling my tea.

"It's as good a place as any I've seen. Strong black community. What are the schools like?"

"Good. Real good!" I said.

"No school today?" Mrs. Roberts asked.

"My wife teaches," Mr. Roberts said apologetically.

"My mother teaches . . . well, she used to." Rebecca ducked her head and took a sip of tea. Mrs. Roberts patted her hand.

"I got to stay home today. I'm at Roper Academy."

"That's a good name for a school."

"It's private," I said, "but not snobby private."

"Do you have a lot of friends there?" Mrs. Roberts asked.

"Feni's too mature for those kids at Roper," Rebecca said proudly. "She likes grown-ups and teenagers. She's quiet. Well, she used to be real quiet."

Ma smiled. "Roper's a good school, Mrs. Roberts. Their teachers are from most every ethnic background with varied teaching concepts. It's a little expensive. My ex-husband and I share the tuition costs."

Mr. and Mrs. Roberts exchanged looks. "Sounds like a nice place to work, Barbara."

"Maybe I ought to look into teaching there. Of course, everything is so up in the air." She waved her hand. "Plenty of time. That's not what we're here to talk about, though," she said, turning to Rebecca. "We came to talk about names."

"Names?" Rebecca and I said at the same time.

"Names for that baby." Mrs. Roberts smiled. "Have you thought about any? Have you thought about religion or anything of the sort? We're both Christian, but the baby wouldn't *have* to be baptized Christian."

"But it's gonna be your baby. How come you asking me about that stuff?"

Mr. Roberts spoke up then. "We've been giving this adoption thing a lot of thought. We thought the right thing to do would be to let you choose a name, maybe religion, too, if you have any interest. 'Course, we want you to know you can come see the baby whenever you please. . . ."

"To visit him? But then he'd know I was his mother!"

"That's your choosing too," Mrs. Roberts said. "We're going to be honest with the baby. . . . Are you sure it's a boy?"

"I have a feeling."

"She didn't get it checked, though," I offered.

"Well, maybe we should think of boy and girl names."

"If it's a girl," Rebecca said quickly, "I want her to be called Afeni."

Mrs. Roberts looked at me and smiled. "Afeni," she said slowly.

I was too surprised to say anything.

"That's Swahili, Mrs. Roberts," Ma said, struggling to keep the pleasure out of her voice. "It means 'the Dear One.' I think that's wonderful, Rebecca."

"Afeni has a pretty sound coming off the tongue, doesn't it?" Mr. Roberts said, repeating my name. "Afeni."

I felt tears in my throat. No one had ever named someone for me before.

"And when he comes out, all plump and dark like his daddy," Rebecca continued, "then I want to call him Daniel."

"Daniel," Mr. Roberts said softly. "That's a strong Bible name, Daniel is."

"He'll have strong fingers if his name is Daniel," I added.

Rebecca and Ma laughed. Daniel had been calling every day for the past month. Rebecca said his mother was going to have his hide when she got her phone bill.

We all sat quietly for a long time, Rebecca smiling at me so much, I nearly started crying. I wanted my grandmother here. She would have liked the Robertses. She would have loved Rebecca.

Twenty-three

THAT NIGHT MARION AND BERNADETTE CAME BY FOR dinner. They had more new clothes for Rebecca and a blanket for the baby. It was white with blue bunnies on it. Rebecca held it to her face and looked at me. "A blanket," she said, and for the first time the baby was real to me.

"I'm sorry I missed the Robertses," Marion said, cutting a piece of vegetable lasagna onto her plate before passing the pan to Bernadette.

"Marion, they are wonderful! She's a teacher!" Ma said.

"A teacher," Marion said, looking over at Rebecca. "That'll make for a smart child."

"They're cool people," Rebecca said. "They didn't make me feel like I was bad or nothing."

"Do we make you feel like that?" Ma asked.

"No way! They're like you, I guess."

"Don't let anyone make you feel like you're bad," Marion warned. "You either, Feni. If they do, send them my way. I have something real *bad* for them!"

Bernadette laughed and leaned over to kiss Marion on the lips. I watched Rebecca's face, but it didn't change.

Under the table she kicked my ankle and I kicked her back.

"This bed rest thing is something else," Marion continued. "I think I brought enough groceries to last about a week."

"You really didn't have to do that, Marion."

"Yes, I did. We told Clair we would do this together, didn't we?"

Ma nodded.

"And it just so happens that it turned out to be easier than any of us expected, so let me do what I need to do." Marion's eyes sparkled behind the thin wire-framed glasses she was wearing.

"How's work going?" Ma asked.

"I have a trial this week that's making me a little crazy," Marion said. "That's why I haven't been here in a while. I'm just wiped out."

"Aren't we all?" Ma agreed. "I still want us all to take that vacation we've been planning for years and years."

"Someday," Bernadette said. "This semester they gave me an English class of seniors! They're so cocky! Rebecca's the best student I have."

"Tell them how I did on the math test," Rebecca said excitedly.

"You tell them, Ms. Rebecca." Bernadette smirked.

"Ninety-two."

"I got a ninety-four on mine," I bragged.

"We're not talking about yours," Rebecca said.

"But we were going to get to it, right, Ma?"

"Anyway," Rebecca continued too loudly, "Bernadette said my math is at twelfth grade now."

"Actually, it's a little higher than that," Bernadette said.

"Beat that!" Rebecca whispered to me.

I rolled my eyes and forked more lasagna onto my plate. "Smarty-pants."

"You two are something else." Marion laughed, shaking her head.

"Ma called again today," Rebecca continued. "She said she's sorry she couldn't take your call last week, Marion, but those nerve pills the doctor gave her make her sleep a lot."

"It's all right. I was planning to try her again on Friday."

"How's she feeling?" Ma asked. "I've been trying to call her too."

"She said my aunt Sylvia is coming to stay with her until I go home."

For the second time that day the thought of Rebecca leaving did a slow, painful dance on my stomach. Underneath the table I wrapped my ankle around hers.

"Ma's gonna be okay," she said.

"She sure is," Marion agreed.

Rebecca looked up at Marion and smiled.

Twenty-four

"I CAN'T BELIEVE BERNADETTE KISSED MARION LIKE that," Rebecca said when we were lying in our beds. It was after midnight, but we were giddy and wide-awake.

"They always do that," I said.

"Bernadette's nice, but she's a little too quiet. She different when she teaches, though. It seems like—like she gets all strong then or something. She sure knows her stuff! I think I learned better here than when I was in Manhattan."

"She's a good teacher."

"You know what, Feni? Marion and your ma would make a nice couple."

"Rebecca!!!"

Rebecca laughed. "Well, they would."

"They're friends."

"That's how it starts out."

"They're like sisters!"

"I know, Feni. I'm just messing with you. Jeez!"

"Anyway, my ma probably won't date anybody else for a long time."

"What makes you say that?"

"Because, soon as Dad left, she stopped drinking. And the people who run the no-drinking programs think you should be sober awhile and work on your own life before you start working on a life with somebody else."

"I guess I can't ever be sober, then."

"You don't drink!"

"Oh. Then I guess I can be sober." Rebecca giggled. "This is such a cool place to be, Feni. You're so lucky." Rebecca got up and came over to my bed. "Move over," she said, and I made space for her. "I like the view of the moon from this side of the room." The bed sank down with the weight of her and the baby. It felt good having company.

"Before you came, Rebecca," I whispered, "the house used to be so quiet. Marion and Bernadette were hardly ever here. It was just me and Ma going about our business."

"You miss the quiet?"

"I didn't know anything else, I guess," I said, putting my hands behind my head and staring up at the ceiling. "I didn't want you to come here. Now I don't want you to go."

"You afraid your house is going to get all quiet again?"

"Yeah."

"I'll give you something that will keep the house from getting quiet and keep you from forgetting me, okay?"

"What is it?" I asked, raising myself up on one elbow.

"This," she said, then her voice dropped.

127

"Against a day of sorrow
Lay by some trifling thing
A smile, a kiss, a promise
For sweet remembering
So when your day is darkest
Without one rift of blue
Take out your little trifle
And dream your dream anew."

After a few minutes had passed in silence, I said, "That's really pretty."

"You have to memorize it. Then when the house gets all quiet, you can say it over and over. Danny taught it to me."

We recited the poem in the darkness until I knew it by heart. Then Rebecca turned and faced the window.

I put my hands behind my head again and recited the poem until I fell asleep.

Twenty-five

"Feni! Feeeeni!" Rebecca screamed from the top of the stairs.

"What?" I screamed back, taking the eggs off the fire and bounding to the stairs. "Rebecca, what?"

It was Friday morning, and I had been in the kitchen making breakfast for us. The Robertses would be by soon to visit Rebecca.

When I got to our room, Rebecca was lying across the bed. The spread was stained with blood. "Call someone," she cried, her face contorted in pain.

I threw a blanket over her and ran to the hall. Ma was at a breakfast meeting outside her office but had left the number on the kitchen wall. Running downstairs, I realized I should call an ambulance first. I turned around and ran back to the top of the stairs, dialed 911, and told them where we were and what was happening. Then I headed for the kitchen again.

Ma picked up on the first ring.

"Ma, it's Feni," I said quickly. "Rebecca's sick, Ma. She's bleeding and everything and I can't find the—"

129

"Slow down," Ma said calmly, and all of a sudden I wanted to cry. "Did you call an ambulance already?"

"Yes."

"Good, then. They should be there soon. Just be calm, Feni. Are you okay?"

"Ma, I'm scared," I whispered.

"Oh, Feni, it'll be okay, sweetheart. I wish I was there with you."

"I wish so too, Ma."

"I'll call Dr. Greenberg and meet you at the hospital. Did you call the Robertses?"

"I'm calling them now."

"I'll call them, Feni. You stay with Rebecca."

"Ma . . . ?"

"She'll be okay, Feni," Ma said.

I hung up the phone and ran back upstairs.

Rebecca was holding the brown doll. Her eyes were closed.

"You can keep the doll, Rebecca. Just don't let anything happen to you," I said, pushing curls out of her face.

"Feni," she whispered, and I moved closer to hear. "Don't let anything happen to little Feni." She took my hand and pressed it against her stomach. Beneath the soft skin, the baby was still.

"Afeni," I said. "I love you, Afeni."

"I love you, Afeni," Rebecca echoed.

In the background the ambulance siren grew closer.

Twenty-six

AFENI ROBERTS CAME INTO THE WORLD AT FOUR-THIRTY
Friday afternoon with soft, wrinkled skin, chocolate-brown
fingers, and Rebecca's wide gray eyes.

"All the rest must be Danny," Ma said, pressing her face
against the nursery window. Marion, the Robertses, and I
were gathered around her, staring down at Afeni. Long and
thin, Afeni lay struggling out of her swaddling between
two sleeping babies, wide-awake.

I watched her silently. She was the reason Rebecca was
here, and she was the reason Rebecca would be leaving
soon. Still, Afeni was not real to me.

Mrs. Roberts sniffed. "Thank you, Jesus," she whispered, reaching for Mr. Roberts's hand. He nodded slowly,
saying nothing.

"That child is going to be something, isn't she?" Marion
said proudly, cooing at the window. "Look at those eyes.
Look how focused she already is."

I felt alone suddenly, far away from everything.

"Can't believe the hardest part is over," Ma said.

But I didn't want it to be over. I didn't want Rebecca to

ever go home. I looked back into the glass and Afeni was staring at me. We stared at each other unblinking until she kicked once, yawned, and closed her eyes.

When the nurse came into the nursery, Ma said, "Why don't you go on up there to see Rebecca, Feni?" and gave me a quick, unexpected hug.

"Aren't you guys coming with me?" I asked.

The Robertses looked at Ma and Marion.

"We'll wait until you two talk. We have time," Mr. Roberts said, taking a seat.

"We have plenty of time." Marion winked, sitting down beside him. "Just like you and Rebecca."

Twenty-seven

"Isn't she something?" Rebecca asked hoarsely.

I nodded, not knowing what to say. All of a sudden I felt like a stranger, a little kid who didn't know anything about having sex or babies.

"It sure was hard, Feni. I don't think I'll ever do it again."

"Did it hurt a lot?"

"You didn't hear me screaming? I thought I woke the dead!"

"No. I didn't hear anything. They made me stay in the waiting room."

Rebecca turned to me, and I stared at her stomach, surprised that it was still big. "What's wrong?"

I shrugged, uncertain.

"I know what it is. You're missing me already, aren't you?"

I nodded and looked at her. Beneath the stark white sheets she looked older and weak.

"Come on, Feni. Soon's I rest a little, we'll really hang out. I'm going to sit in on your classes and blow those Roper kids away. I'm gonna say I'm a new kid."

"Really?"

"Then I want to go to Jake's and Joe's."

"Jack and Jill, Rebecca." I laughed. "Jack and Jill!"

"Then maybe we can go back to where those shacks are and see that girl. Remember her?"

"How could I forget?"

"See, nothing's changed, Feni. I'm just going to be moving a lot faster."

I felt better then. Nothing *had* changed between us.

"Danny called twice," Rebecca said.

"Yeah. I called him to give him your number here. He sure has a nice voice."

"And a nice everything else to go with it."

I laughed.

Rebecca was leaning back against three pillows, wearing the blue-and-white-striped dressing gown Marion had bought her. Her cheeks looked thinner now and the dimples were small permanent half-moons. A stack of magazines rested on the table next to her bed. Beside them sat a box of tissues and a pitcher of water. Blue elves ran across the television screen.

"So is this what you'll be doing here all day?" I asked, lifting a magazine and dropping it down again.

"Mostly. I guess I'll feed and talk to Afeni."

"You gonna breast-feed her?"

"For a little while. Everyone thinks it'll be okay. Then maybe I can get these things back down to size," she said, holding her breasts in her hands.

"She's not hard to look at at all, Rebecca."

"What do you mean 'not hard to look at'? That is the most beautiful baby in that whole nursery!"

"Okay," I teased. "Maybe she is a little cute."

Rebecca sucked her teeth. "Man, you better grow some eyes. You see that pretty nose and those ears?" She laughed. "Those are her daddy's ears!"

"But she has your eyes."

"They might not stay that color. Babies change like that. Sometimes they come out light skinned, then two days later, zap, dark and sweet as a berry."

"Really?"

"Yup," Rebecca said. "Sometimes they have gray or blue eyes for a day or two and then, next thing you know, they're little brown-eyed girls!"

"Well, we'll just have to see. You gonna stay around for the changes, right?" I asked hopefully.

"I don't know how much longer I'll be here. Maybe until the end of the month. Then I have to go home. I miss my family so much. Yesterday Bobo and Shaunney called me. They wanted to tell me that they know their two-times tables. So then they recited them for me over and over again until my ma got on and asked how I was doing and all that stuff, then said they couldn't afford to talk any longer. I miss Ma."

"I wish you could live with us, Rebecca. I wish you could stay forever!"

"I'll be back to visit, you know. I like Seton. The other night, when we were lying in bed, I was thinking. We're gonna grow up and do what we have to do, and we're gonna be so different from each other just because of where we live."

"I don't want us to forget each other."

"You crazy?" Rebecca said. "How could I forget a brat like you?"

"How could I forget a pain like you?"

We laughed for a long time, then grew silent, staring up at the TV screen until the nurse came in with Rebecca's dinner: fish.

"Remember *fishes*?"

"Oh, I hated you that day," Rebecca said, and we laughed until she coughed. I patted her back and held the plastic cup of water to her lips. Rebecca took a small sip, then looked at me for a long time. "Thank you," she said softly.

A few minutes after dinner the nurse brought Afeni in for her feeding, and I watched as her tiny mouth searched for Rebecca's breast. I stared at the small eyes for a long time.

"She looks a little like an elf, doesn't she?" I asked, giving Afeni my finger to hold on to.

"Hey, Elf," Rebecca whispered, kissing her forehead.

"Elf beats Stinky any day, doesn't it?"

Rebecca looked up at me and smiled. "Anything beats Stinky!"

I stared at Baby Afeni's tiny fingers. In that moment I knew that she, like me and Ma and Rebecca and Marion and Clair and Bernadette and especially my grandmother, was another part of a long line of dear ones. No one knew yet if she'd be light or dark, gap toothed or dimpled; if her hair would be kinky, curly, or straight; no one knew if she'd find her roots back to Harlem or settle in Seton, or whether or not she'd hate Jack and Jill and White Gloves and Manners; but we were certain of one thing—through the toughest, the saddest, the hardest, and the best of times, all of us would be around somewhere, pulling for her and pulling her through.

Downstairs, Ma and Marion and the Robertses were waiting for me and Rebecca to finish talking. They were waiting for the moment when they could come upstairs to coo over Baby Afeni some more and be reminded of other babies in their lives. They were waiting for Rebecca and me to say good-bye to each other, not knowing if our paths would ever cross again. They were waiting for the time to come when they could sit back in rocking chairs and remember this, hold on to it, and tell it to their grandchildren.

But most of all they were waiting for us to grow up and wondering if we'd grow into Marions, Catherines, or Clairs.

"What are you standing there with your mouth open for, Feni? Go downstairs and get the gang!"

In her own words

Jacqueline Woodson shares some thoughts and insights about
the dear one

Where it takes place:
In Pennsylvania in the fictionalized town of Seton.

Where I wrote it:
In Harlem, New York, and in Brooklyn, New York.

Why I wrote it:
The Dear One was the second novel I ever wrote. I wanted to write about teenage pregnancy. At the time I was working with runaway and homeless young people—many of whom were pregnant. I wanted to write a novel that spoke to them.

ABOUT HERSELF:

What's your favorite color?
Blue, sometimes green but mostly blue.

What's your favorite food?
Pizza.

What foods don't you like?
Avocado, mushrooms, artichokes, raspberries, papaya, meat, brussels sprouts, alfalfa sprouts, oatmeal . . . This list is actually much longer, but I'll stop here.

DO YOU HAVE BROTHERS AND SISTERS?

I have an older brother and an older sister and a younger brother. Even though I'm five feet ten inches tall, I'm the shortest person in my family.

WHERE WERE YOU BORN?

Columbus, Ohio, but I spent my early life in Greenville, South Carolina. We moved to Brooklyn when I was about seven.

WHAT WAS YOUR FAVORITE SUBJECT IN SCHOOL?

I loved English and anything where we got to do writing. I was terrible at math and science. I loved gym and Spanish and anything that allowed us to dance or jump around. I wasn't a big fan of sitting still too long unless I was reading. I always read the same books again and again.

WHAT ARE/WERE SOME OF YOUR FAVORITE BOOKS?

As a kid, I loved anything by Virginia Hamilton or Judy Blume. I also loved *The Selfish Giant* by Oscar Wilde and *The Little Match Girl* by Hans Christian Andersen. Oh— and *Stevie* by John Steptoe. These days, I feel like my favorites list grows and grows. A sampling of the authors and illustrators I love: Chris Raschka, Chris Lynch, Chris Myers—and not because they all have the same name! I also love An Na, Karen Hesse, Kashmira Sheth, Mildred Taylor, James Baldwin, Anne Lamott, Rosa Guy, Christopher Paul Curtis, Walter Dean Myers, Hope Anita Smith, Carson McCullers, Raymond Carver, Audre Lorde. . . . I could go on and on.

WHY DO YOU LOVE WRITING SO MUCH?

Because it makes me happy. Even when the words are slow in coming and the story seems all lopsided, writing keeps me happy.

WHERE HAVE YOU TRAVELED?

I've been to all fifty states and met some really cool young people in all of them. I've been to England, France, Germany, Puerto Rico, Belize, Virgin Gorda, and Mexico. And probably a couple of other places I don't remember right now.

WHAT LANGUAGES DO YOU SPEAK?

Mostly English but I also know Spanish and a good bit of American Sign Language. If I am desperate, I can find a bathroom in French and German.

WHAT ARE SOME OF THE OTHER LANGUAGES YOUR BOOKS ARE PUBLISHED IN?

Italian, Dutch, Tagalog, French, Spanish, German, Japanese, Mandarin, Turkish, and a few others I don't remember right now.

IS WRITING HARD?

Yes. Anything you do that you want to do well can be difficult at times. Revising is hard. Thinking of new things to write about is hard. And the difficulty makes it that much more rewarding.

Are any of your books based on your life?

The only ones that have some autobiographical content are *Visiting Day*, *Sweet, Sweet Memory*, *Show Way*, and all the Maizon books.

Do you ever get writer's block?

Nope. I don't believe there is any such thing as writer's block. I think it's just your mind telling you that the thing you're writing isn't the thing you really want to be writing. If this happens to me, I start writing something else.

Do you have any kids?

I have a daughter named Toshi and a son named Jackson-Leroi. Toshi was named after her godmom, Toshi Reagon, who is a really cool singer.

What was your first job?

When I was a toddler, I did a series of advertisements for Alaga Syrup in *Ebony* magazine. Even though I was only two, I looked a lot older, and the ads that ran often featured me as a school-aged child thinking about Alaga Syrup. I don't remember loving it. But it was technically my first job.

What music do you listen to?

Here are some of the people on my computer: Toshi Reagon, Joni Mitchell, Kanye West, Talib Kweli, Bruce Springsteen, Black Eyed Peas, Nas, Indigo Girls, ani difranco, Eminem, and the whole *Free to Be . . . You and Me* soundtrack.

HOW MANY BOOKS DO YOU WORK ON AT ONE TIME?

I'm usually working on two or three books at once. When I get bored with one, or get stuck, I go on to the other one.

WHERE DO YOU WRITE?

I have a writing room in my house in Brooklyn. Sometimes I go to a place called The Writers Room in Manhattan. Sometimes I sit on the stoop or write in Prospect Park. Sometimes, if an idea starts coming, I just write wherever I am and on whatever I have.

OF ALL THE BOOKS YOU'VE WRITTEN, DO YOU HAVE A FAVORITE?

Nope. I like each of them for different reasons. Sometimes, long after I've finished a book, I'm still thinking about the people in them.

IF YOU COULDN'T WRITE, WHAT WOULD YOU DO?

Play for the NBA—try to make those Knicks a winning team!

DO YOU THINK YOU'LL EVER STOP WRITING?

When I stop breathing.

Turn the page for a sample
of **JACQUELINE WOODSON**'s
Newbery Honor book

After Tupac
and D Foster

The summer before D Foster's real mama came and took her away, Tupac wasn't dead yet. He'd been shot five times—two in the head, two down by his leg and thing and one shot that went in his hand and came out the other side and went through a vein or something. All the doctors were saying he should have died and were bringing other doctors up to his room to show everybody what a medical miracle he was. That's what they called him. A Medical Miracle. Like he wasn't even a real person. Like he was just something to be looked at and turned this way and that way and poked at. Like he wasn't Tupac.

D Foster showed up a few months before Tupac got shot that first time and left us the summer before he died. By the time her mama came and got her and she took one last walk on out of our lives, I felt like we'd grown up and grown old and lived a hundred lives in those few years that we knew her. But we hadn't really. We'd just gone from being eleven to being thirteen. Three girls. Three the Hard Way. In the end, it was just me and Neeka again.

The first time Tupac got shot, it was November 1994. Cold as anything everywhere in the city and me, Neeka, D and everybody else was shivering our behinds through the winter with nobody thinking Pac was gonna make it. Then, right after he had some surgery, he checked himself out of the hospital even though the doctors was trying to tell him he wasn't well enough to be doing that. That's when everybody around here started talking about what a true gangsta he was. At least that's what all the kids were thinking. The churchgoing people just kept saying he had God with him. Some of the parents were saying what they'd always been saying about him—that he was heading right to what he got because he was a bad example for kids, especially black kids like us. Crazy stuff about Tupac being a disgrace to the race and blah, blah, blah. The wannabe gangsta kids just kept saying Tupac was gonna get revenge on whoever did that to him.

But when I saw Tupac like that—coming out of the hospital, all skinny and small-looking in that wheelchair, big guards around him—I remember thinking, *He ain't gonna try to get revenge on nobody and he ain't trying to be a disgrace to anybody either. Just trying to keep on.* Even though he wasn't smiling, I knew he was just happy and confused about still being alive.

Went on like that all winter long, then February came and they sent Tupac to jail for some dumb stuff and people started talking about that—the negative peeps talking about that's where he needed to be and all the rest of us saying how messed up the law was when you didn't look and act like people thought you should.

Spring came and Pac dropped his album from prison and this one song on it was real tight, so we all just listened to it and talked about how bad-ass Pac was—that he wasn't even gonna let being in jail stop him from making his music. Me and Neeka and D had all turned twelve by then, but we still believed stuff—like that we'd grow up and marry beautiful rapper guys who'd buy us huge houses out in the country. We talked about how they'd be all crazy over us and if some other girl walked by who was fine or something, they wouldn't even turn their heads to look because they'd be so in love with us and all. Stupid stuff like that.

In jail, Pac started getting clear about thug life, saying it wasn't the right thing. He got all *righteous* about it and whatnot, and with all the rappers shooting on each other and stuff, it wasn't hard to agree with him.

3

Time kept passing on that way. Things and people changing. First, D turned thirteen, then me and Neeka were right
there behind her—us all turning into teenagers, getting body,
getting tall, boys acting stupid over us.

Seems soon as we started settling into all that changing,
D's mama came—took her away from us.

And time kept on creeping.

Then Tupac went and died and it got me thinking about
D. About the short time she was with us and about how you
could know somebody real good but not know them at the
same time. And it made me want to remember. Yeah, I guess
that's it. I guess that's what I'm trying to do now. . . .